Leather and Shoe Finishing

Raghubar Dayal Singh

First published in India in 2017 by Invincible Publishers

ISBN: 978-93-86148-95-7

Publisher:
Invincible Publishers
G-120, Shushant Lok III
Sector 57, Gurgaon-122001
Phone: +91 124 4273677, +91 9599667779

This book dedicated to my beloved parents (Mother Late Smt. Kalawati Singh & Father Shree Ishwar Dayal Singh).

CONTENTS

f- Patent finish
g- Burnished finish
h- Brush- off finish
i- Oil- pull up finish
j- Crazy horse finish
k- Nubuck/ suede finish
l- Laminated finish

Chapter – 4

TYPES OF LEATHERS WHICH MAY BE ENCOUNTERED IN FINISHING-

a- Casual aniline leather
b- Slightly corrected grain leather
c- Box and willow sides
d- Semi- aniline or mock aniline leather
e- Corrected grain box and willow uppers
f- Printed leather with aniline look
g- Normal glazed finish box and willow upper
h- Goat glazed leather.

Chapter – 5

POLYURETHANE EMULSION FOR LEATHER FINISHES-

Chapter – 6

LEATHER TESTING

Introduction

1- Physical Test- Grain strength, Tear strength, Tensile strength

2- Chemical test- Chrome content, Fat content, Mineral salt content, Pentachlorophenol test.
3- Finish Test- Finished adhesion, Flex resistance, rub fastness test.
4- General chemicals like tanning agent test.
5- Microscopic and bacteriological test.
6- Color matching and CAD/ CAM

SHOE FINISHING

Chapter – 6

SHOE FINISHING

1- Introduction
2- Function of shoe finishing
3- Grouping of leather type for finishing purposes

Chapter -7

SHOE FINISHING PROCESS

1- Cleaning- Objects and principles, Types of cleaners, Application of cleaners, Methods of cleaning.
2- Repairing- Objects and principles, Repairing crayons, Repairing paste, Precautions taken.
3- Wrinkle Chasing- Machine operations, Ironing, Hot air blower, Boot leg treeing machine, Precautions taken.
4- Filling by base coat application- Use of fillers- Light, Medium and Heavy fillers and their application process.
5- Dressing- Types of dressing and their applications, Types of dressing water base and solvent base.
6- Top coat applications.

Chapter -8

CREAM, POLISHERS & WAXES

1- Introduction of cream and polishers
2- Application procedures

3- Use of waxes in shoe finishing operation
4- Abrasive wax and their characteristics
5- Repairing wax and their characteristics- soft and hard wax.
6- Burnishing wax and their application with burnishing machine
7- Protectors
8- Brush off finish
9- Antique finish
10- Shadow finish
11- Treatment on leather upper
12- Treatment on synthetic upper
13- Basic problems encountered in the upper finishing.

Chapter – 9

MATERIAL, TOOLS AND EQUIPMENTS USED IN SHOE FINISHING OPERATIONS-

1- Soap and Detergent
2- Solvent cleaners
3- Polishers
4- Conditioners
5- Policing wax
6- Top coat polish
7- Repairing wax
8- Repairing crayons
9- Repairing paste
10- Uniformers, renovators
11- Sole Edge color , their features and direction
12- Base coat polish
13- Bottom or sole finish, Leather sole and heel finish
14- Nubuck and suede care and sprays
15- Liquid polish, polishing instructions, tips and tricks
16- Emery paper

PREFACE

Finished leather enriches our lives in numerous pleasant ways. The belts and shoes that we wear and the wallets and purses that we carry are made of finished leather. This transformation has been made possible primarily due to the induction of state- of- the- art treatment and latest technologies to give leather a never- before – possible thickness, unlimited color variations, tones, luxurious feel and silky touch.

In footwear and leather garments market every season with its fashion changes, brings worries to manufacturer and retailer who have to select new ranges of footwear or leather goods. They want, the product having sales appeal, the right price, least production problem and satisfactory wear performance. So, every footwear or leather goods finished products should maintain fit assessment, visual assessment, and laboratory test and wear test.

Footwear is more than a simple wrapping or protection of the foot. The notation that shoes indicate a great deal about a person's taste and identity- national, regional, professional – class status and gender, is not an invention of modernity. Shoes have, for centuries, given hints about a person's character, social and cultural place, even sexual preference. Shoes are powerful things as they take control over the physical and human space in which we live.

Leather or shoe finishing is a process of up- gradation and it hide the grain defect, so it occurs the value addition for the customer, by improving the aesthetic. Actually a good finishing provides appeal to the shoes and develops brand loyalty. It provides the value addition of the final product.

The up- grading of leather in simple terms means – to make the best leather possible out of the available crust material. This includes the highest quality as well as the largest cutting yield while keeping the elegance and natural aspect of the final leather. Since the gap between the supply and demand of high class raw material is increasing rather than decreasing, up- grading becomes more and more important. For more of the shoe upper leathers the technologies are no alternatives, because these leathers do not have thick finishing layers, so up-grading has to be achieved with thin coats. Different defects in different sizes and on different leathers need different up- grading techniques and product systems.

To achieve a smooth and even surface and sufficient cutting yield, the leather needs to be well prepared before applying the best coat. Very common today is the pre- treatment of the crust with microspheres – containing pre- base products by reverse roller coating. This can be done either on the full grain crust and the subsequent buffing will then remove the surplus and even out the surface in terms of up-grading.

This book will be great help to the leather & Footwear industry especially in finishing department, both in unorganized as well as organized sector, in recognition of the importance of working procedures, applications, quality control and quality inspection. The book **"Leather and shoe finishing"** is being published for the benefit of Leather and Footwear industry. My mission is to provide world class education that the young men and women capable of assuming leadership of the society for the betterment of the footwear and leather industry.

R. D. Singh

B. Tech. (Leather) M.B.A. (POM)

Junior Consultant (Footwear)

F.D.D.I. Kolkata (W.B.) Campus.

ACKNOWLEDGEMENT

This book is result of team work – a team of people who have supported me, directly or indirectly. I am grateful to all my well-wishers, students, and colleagues – past and present, who have helped me a lot in shaping my thought process. In, particular, I express my sincere thanks to Mrs. Satyam Srivastava mam, Sr. Consultant (Footwear) for her important contributions.

I am thankful to my friends and family members, especially my father and mother in law Dr. H. N. Singh and Mrs. Indu Singh who always encouraged me to keep the spirit high during the really tough periods of long continuous work. I am grateful to my wife Sandhya Singh, kids – Richa, Charvi and Prakhar for their lovable support, without their support this book would not have been possible.

I am extremely grateful to Hon. Managing Director of Footwear Design & Development Institute Shree Sameer Kumar Srivastava I.R.S., Senior Executive Director of Kolkata campus Shree Vikash Singh I.R.S. and all the senior management of FDDI family for their help and co- operation.

I am highly indebted to Mr. Samuel Chakroborty, Center Head, FDDI Kolkata campus, all the H.O.D. of various branches, my colleagues for their initiating and helping me in this work. Without their personal involvement, even the beginning the work on the book not have been possible.

Last, but not the least, my sincere thanks are also due to various individuals and organizations for beings the source of examples, illustrations and cases included in the book. Illustrations and cases have been included with the sole purpose of aiding class discussion, and without these the book could not have come out in the present form. I have tried my best to acknowledge all the sources at relevant places throughout the book, as accurately as possible. I must mention that the limitations, short comings or mistakes that might have remained in the book are entirely mine.

I also acknowledge the inputs and support received from all my students, especially Mr. Neel Kamal Panday, Durgesh Chandra, Aditya Singh, Prasoon, Niyata, Aditi, Medha, Babita and Neha.

I also wish to thanks to readers in anticipations of their comments and suggestions. I can be reached at rdsingh@fddiindia.com or rdayalsingh1961@gmail.com.

R. D. Singh

Jr. Consultant (Footwear)

ABOUT THE AUTHOR

Raghubar Dayal Singh
B. Tech. (Leather Tech.) Kanpur University (U. P.)
M.B.A. (POM in Footwear) UPRTOU Allahabad (U.P.)
Highlights of the Industrial Exposure & Qualifications-

1- 36 years of professional and Industrial background in Leather, Footwear, Industrial consultancy, quality system and training.

2- B. Tech. Leather Technology by qualification.

3- M.B.A. (Production Operation Management) from U. P. Rajarshi Tondon University, Allahabad (U. P.) India.

4- Examiner and paper setter of U. P. Technical Board Lucknow (U. P.) . Examiner No- 240017.

PROFESSIONAL QUALIFICATION

B. Tech. in Leather Technology (4 years Degree Course) from Harcourt Butler Technological Institute, (H. B. T. I.) Kanpur (U. P.) India affiliated to Kanpur University in 1983 for the following courses.

- **Industrial Management**
- **Theory & Practice of Leather Manufacturing.**
- **Footwear and Leather good manufacturing.**

- **Leather Equipment design & Drawing.**

M.B.A. (Production Operation Management) from U. P. Rajarshi Tondon Open University, Allahabad (U. P.) India with 85% marks.

In 36 years journey he worked outside India for several years as a Production Manager and as a Consultant (Leather & Footwear) in a well reputed export organization.

Beside above the undersigned to Italy, Germany, Pakistan, Nepal and Ethiopia for training, quality improvement and cost saving in Polyurethane finish with water base resin and other finishes etc. on the latest Technology as well as machineries.

From 2008 till date working in Footwear Design and Development Institute (FDDI) affiliated to Ministry of Commerce and Industry, Govt. of India as a Junior Consultant in Footwear Department.

ARTICLE PUBLISHED-

S. No.	Publisher	Topic	Year	Single/ combined
1-	Footwear Digest	Identification of important areas of research in tanning industry.	October 2010	Single
2-	Footwear Digest	Chrome tanning and its environmental impact.	2011	Single
3-	Footwear Today	Industrial & Trade Development Policy	2012	Single
4-	Fiber 2 fashion.com	Leather and the environment	2012	Single
5-	Fiber2fashion.com	The art and science of footwear design	2013	Single
6-	Fiber2fashion.com	Total Quality Management	2014	single
7-	Vivodh	Footwear with jute (as a golden fiber)	2014	Single

FINISHING OF LEATHER

The term **"leather finishing"** relates to those operations which give the leather its final appearance and make it useful, attractive and appealing to its user. Finishes- on leather also serve as a protective coating.

The wide variety of colored pigments, binders, waxes etc. applied to the leather are known as finishes. Both the composition and application of these are varied to suit the requirement of the end product, not only in terms of color, gloss, handle, resistance to wear, solvents, heat, flexing, rubbing etc. but also in terms of uniformity of surface appearance.

The natural surface of leather is not uniform in appearance and this often constitutes its natural appeal relative to plastics and other substitute materials.

The non- uniformity of surface appearance in any one skin or a pack of skins may be such as to render it unsuitable for a particular purpose. Hence we say that uniformity of color may be a function of tanning, dyeing etc. and be so satisfactory that the finishing process only involves mechanical operations of polishing, brushing, embossing etc as required.

Finishing in general has got four fold objectives-

1- Protection
2- Decoration
3- Physical characteristics
4- Up- gradation

1- PROTECTION- It protect against dry and wet rub test, acid, alkali etc. fungas spray or silicon pockets are used for protection of leather from moisture.

2- DECORATION- We can provide two tone effect, multi- color effect, multi- design, gloss etc. for their special appearance.

3- PHYSICAL CHARACTERISTICS- The characteristics like flexural endurance, degree of brightness, special effects like- shadowing, antiquing, durability of finish in wear, water resistance, feel etc.

4- **UP- GRADATION-** Up- gradation can be started as a 4th dimension of leather finishing because while the available hide and skins are 80 to 90% defective and also their supply limited, the demand of quality goods is ever increasing.

For using the best finishing auxiliaries and the proper suitable mechanical operations all are achieved by the following-

----- Degree of brightness

----- Proper waxy feel

----- Special effect

----- Cleanliness- Lack of marks and flaws

----- Durability of the finish in wear

Hence the finishing of leather is very important as for as the final appearance and surface properties are concerned. This appearance deals with the art of improving the quality of the crust leather so as to make it suitable for the manufacture of footwear or other leather goods.

Finishing may improve the quality of leather in so for as

1- **Levelness of color on the skin**

2- **Uniformity of shade from skin to skin and pack to pack**

3- **Changing the color as per need**

4- **Adding a transparent film though which the natural appearance of the leather may be viewed.**

OBJECTIVE OF FINISHING-

The main objective of finishing is-

1- To provide surface coating so as to protect the leather from damage due to rubbing and scratching.

2- To give level appearance of color.

3- To give suitable shade as per the fashion demands.

4- To retain its properties during the all shoe making operations and could be easily dressed to cover up the machine cuts and abrasions.

PROPERTIES OF IDEAL FINISHING FILM-

Leathers are subjected to various mechanical stress and strain during operation. In order that the finishing coats on leather can also stand the severe mechanical handling they should satisfy the following physicochemical requirements.

1- An elongation adequate to maintain the coating when the leather is stretched to the maximum permissible degree.
2- A modulus of elasticity in line with the hardness of the coating.
3- Stability against repeated tensile and compressive strains and bending, means it should not crack on being extended or flexed.
4- Elasticity, ensuring that the coating will return to its original condition when the deforming forces no longer act.
5- Resistant to heat, cold and moisture.
6- Durability against rubbing on dry and wet leather.
7- Should be fast to stain and light.
8- Should be easily cleaned and polished.
9- High adhesion.
10- Permeability to water vapor and air , ensuring the hygienic properties of leather.

PREPARATION OF THE LEATHER BEFORE FINISHING-

Before finishing, the leather should be sorted out to examine their nature in order that correct formulation of leather finish, the application method and the drying conditions are carefully determined.

The desirable characteristics of leather prior to finishing operations are-

1- The leather should have a flat, smooth grain with a fine break, tight flanks and even substance.
2- The grain surface should not be excessively greasy. Greasy grains will cause inadequate finish, poor coverage and a streaky appearance. In addition, the fat migrates to the finish layer when the leather is subsequently hot plated.

3- The leather meant for corrected- grain finish should have a uniform buffed surface.

4- The leather should not be too absorptive.

5- The leather must be well laid out to facilitate brushing, padding and spraying operations.

ABSORPTIVE QUALITY OF LEATHER-

One of the most important factors which require careful study in finishing of leather especially corrected- grain upper leather is the absorbability of the leather towards finishing solution. Absorptive quality depends on-

a) Nature and extent of retanning. The leather becomes increasingly absorptive with the increase of the degree of retanning with vegetable, synthetic or resin tanning materials. Use of excessive masking salts in chrome tanning can also cause this defect.

b) Extent of drying prior to and during finishing.

c) Depth of buffing the grain surface.

Excessive absorbency may cause a grey cast and a harsh feel and necessitates larger additions of binders leading to coarse break and also uneven shade.

The varying absorptive quality of the leather surface should be leveled up and the surface sealed with mixtures of plasticizers, emulsified oils, cationic oil ground and similar products. In this way a very efficient sealing effect is obtained by providing a plasticized cover to the opened-up grain structure and by producing some degree of water repellency on the leather surface.

STRUCTURE OF FINISH FILM-

The finish film is structured basically in three layers-

1- Bottom Layer or ground coat

2- Intermediate Layer or middle coat

3- Top Layer or final coat

1- **BOTTOM LAYER OR GROUND COAT-** The object of bottom coat is to fill and cover the opened- up surface of the leather, to seal together the leather fibers exposed due to buffing operation and so contribute towards enhancing the strength of the finish film. It is also meant to level up the varying absorptive property of the leather surface and even up the shade desired in the final leather. In many cases the ground coat is also expected to act as a plasticizer reservoir. As for as possible, the bottom coat should be designed to cover faults.

It is the first layer having the following properties-

a) It provides the base to the intermediate layer for better adhesion with leather.

b) It is soft film & well plasticized.

c) Its PH is in between 6 to 7.

d) It gives good filling effect.

e) This layer is responsible for covering the defects and giving surface uniformity.

2- **INTERMEDIATE LAYER OR MIDDLE COAT-**

The middle coat is intended to be a covering and leveling coat so that any finishing marks or grain defects can be eliminated and covered at this stage. By adding various proportions of lust ring and matting agents the desired degree of gloss is adjusted. To obtain increased resistance to hot plating and also to confer a more leathery feel higher proportions of albumin and lower proportions of resin binder binder are added in the middle coat.

It is the middle layer having the following properties-

a) The intermediate layer covers major portion of the finish film thickness.

b) It is harder than the bottom layer.

c) It has got holding power for pigments etc.

3- TOP LAYER OR FINAL COAT-

The final coat which is usually free from resin is designed to increase fastness to wet and dry rubbing and also help to obtain adequate resistance to hot plating. Small quantities of wax preparations are also used to obtain a warm feel and the best possible surface smoothness. Gloss can be controlled in a suitable manner by the

The finishing coats are hardened with diluted formaldehyde or mixture of formaldehyde and chrome solution. Hardening also has a decisive influence upon the resistance to hot plating.

The top layer has got the following properties-

a) Gives required gloss and attractive appearance.

b) Protects the intermediate layer from scratch and other frictional damages.

c) In some cases makes the finish film waterproof and resistant to mild chemicals.

d) Gives the surface of the leather resistant enough to withstand the temperature and pressure of plating.

TYPES OF FINISHES (SYSTEM)

Broadly there are two systems of finishes-

1- **AQUEOUS FINISH-** Protein binder, Acrylic resins, Lacquer emulsions etc. come under this category.

2- **NON-AQUEOUS FINISH-** Vinyl resin finish, Nitrocellulose lacquer, PVC lacquer, PU finish etc. come under this category.

Non- aqueous finishes	**Aqueous finishes**
1. Good gloss, Abrasive resistance	1. Poor glass (except protein finish) rest Color fastness, Resistant to water properties is poor comparatively & other chemicals.
2.Poor comparatively	2. Better water vapour permeability, Resistant to organic solvents.
3. Better antifungal effects	3. Poor comparatively.
4. Toxic & inflammable	4. Not this type.
5. Dust free atmosphere required.	5. Dust free atmosphere required
6. Costly process	6. Cheaper

FINISHING MATERIALS-

PIGMENTS-

Pigments play a very important role of present day in leather finishing compositions. The use of pigments in the finishing of leather had its start in America during World War 1. Because the supply of dyestuffs from Germany was cut off. While pigmented finishes lacked the brilliance and beauty of finishes base on dyestuffs, they had the advantages of covering stains and defects and presenting a uniform color over the whole skin or hide. This advantage becomes more and more important as time went on increasing amount of buffed side leather and decreasing amount of full grain calf being finished. As a result, even when dyestuffs become available again the use of pigments was never given up. Glazed kid is finished with aniline finishes, as a number of novelty leathers also. In a general way, however the big volume leathers are finished with coatings which contain pigments.

Great progress has been made by the manufacturers of dry pigments since the early days of pigment finishing when the naturally occurring earth pigments were used. Virtually all the pigments used today in the finishing of leather are chemically produced with a very high degree of reproducibility of shade and strength, and with a minimum of muddiness of color.

Particular progress has been made in the field of organic pigments, toners and lakes- many of which gives essentially the brilliance of the day used in their manufacture and at the same time a reasonably good degree of hiding power.

The pigments normally used in leather finishes are as follow-

White - **Titanium oxide**

Black - **Carbon black, bone black, iron oxide**

Yellow - **Lead chromate, cadmium sulphide- selenide, iron oxide**

Orange - **Lead chromate**

Brown - **Iron oxide**

Blue - **Phthalocyanin green, chrome green**

Red - **Cadmium sulfide- selenides, organic lakes and toners.**

While some tanners still makes their own pigment dispersion, most now purchase them from companies who make a specialty of manufacturing such pigment dispersion in addition to various other products for leather finishing uses. The pigments are dispersed in a vehicle using some kind of mill which does not work of breaking up the pigment agglomerates into the original fine particles that existed before the pigments was dried down.

The pigment must be stable to heat, so that discoloration will not occur during hot processing operations at the tannery or shoe factory. They must also have good light stability, so that the colours do not fade and they should also be free from bleeding into subsequent coats. These problems are particularly acute in red, so very great care has to be taken in the selection of red pigments.

DYESTUFFS-

Dyestuffs are used quite widely in the aqueous finish coats on certain leather, particularly shoe leather. On full aniline leather they are of course, the only coloring materials present. For aniline calf it will seen that in the first coat basic dyes are used simply diluted with water containing a small amount of acetic or formic acid , while the subsequent finish coats contain acid or direct dyes in conjunction with casein, carnauba wax and shellac.

Basic dyes can not be used in conjunction with protein solutions, so as normally in pigment finishes only acid dyes are used if dyes are used at all. They provide brilliance in pigment finishes, and the higher the ratio of acid dye to pigment, the more aniline is the final appearance and of course, the poorer the covering. While combination of acid dye and aqueous dispersed pigments are widely used in the finishing of shoe side leathers, this approach is generally avoided in upholstery leather where complete resistance to cracking, bleeding and fading is demanded.

AQUEOUS BINDERS-

While many leathers are finished with essentially pigments and resin dispersions in the underneath coats, other leathers including the all important shoe side leather, make use of a variety of additional binding materials and auxiliary materials as well. In some process, some side leather are making with " simple finishes" such as ammonia- casein, borax- shellac, and carnauba wax. Instead most of them buy prepared binders from companies who specialize in making leather finishes. These binders are solid under trade names or numbers and there is such a variety of products of this nature that it is impossible to classify them in any clear cut way. Some are hard, some are waxy, and some contains resins in addition to the other water- soluble or water dispersed materials. Some are referred to as glazing binders and are used on those leathers which are friction glazed, although some of the calf skin tanners still prepare simple glazing seasons in their own tanneries using casein, egg-albumen and blood albumen as constituents. Other are referred to as plating binders and are used as additional to resins and pigment dispersions to assist application to facilitate smooth plating to produce gloss or to give additional filling, smoothness and desirable surface feel to the finish.

Protein (particularly casein) waxes (such as carnauba wax, bees wax and montan wax) and natural resins (such as shellac) are probably present as constituents of some of these binders. In addition to the natural binders such as casein there are also now available hard binders in aqueous solution base on acrylic resins into which hydrophilic groups have been built to confer water solubility. These when dried down are more water resistant than casein film.

AQUEOUS AUXILIARY MATERIALS-

In addition to synthetic resin dispersions, pigment dispersion, dyes and a variety of aqueous binders may other materials are used in aqueous finish systems in order to produce satisfactory surface coatings. Thickeners are used to control the degree of penetration and are particularly useful on very open absorbent surface such as splits. Leveling agents are widely used in many finish mixtures which are applied by brushing machine. These have the property of lowering the surface tension of the finish mixture which permits the slight ridges in the wet finish to flow out better, thus helping to prevent streaking. Many antifoaming agents are also used in water finishes. These are particularly useful in finishes which are applied by seasoning machines in which the finish is subjected to continual vigorous agitation by the brush and by the circulating pump. Dulling agents are used, mostly in the top coats to control the gloss.

EGG AND BLOOD ALBUMIN-

87.5% water. In leather finishing it is used for seasoning light leather where a high gloss is required like glazed kid, chrome calf.

Albumin solution takes a high polish but has poor grain-filling properties. Blood albumins are derived from cattle slaughterhouse which is allowed to clot and the serum separated from the red corpuscles. The separated serum is then dried in shallow vessels at low temperature. In leather industry the whole blood of cattle is frequently used in black or heavier shade of brown leather finishing. Blood albumin, like egg albumin produces high gloss when leathers are friction glazed but the use of too much should be avoided.

SHELLAC-

These are the natural resin obtained from "Lac" and are used for glazed finish. Waterproofing properties can be incorporated if shellac is treated with ammonia or Borax. Shellac gives a type of brittle film.

OILS FATS AND WAXES-

All oil, fats and waxes have lubricating properties. This statement indicates that they promote the slipping of adjacent surfaces against each other or reduce the adhesion between them. This is the fundamental process of application which governs the gross-penetration of the oil into the inter fiber spaces and also the manner in which the oil molecules are attached to the molecular structure of the leather fabrils.

Waxes are the sub-group of the class of fatty materials which are not greasy to the touch, and which do not contain glycerol combined with the fatty acid. The definition tends to be loose i,e, spearm oil is chemically a wax, whilst paraffin wax is chemically a pure hydrocarbon oil. The plants waxes are obtained from the outer surface of the leaves, fruits, flowers or streams of plants.

There are different types of waxes used in leather and footwear industry-

1- PARAFFIN WAX-

Melting point = 35 to 56 degree c

Paraffin wax is a white wax from which cheap white candles are made, and can be obtained in qualities with different melting point. It behaves like a wax and is used in the cheaper type of polish; it is chemically not classed as a wax. If it is mixed with chrome and sole leather. In leather finishes it is emulsified with water and an emulsifying agent to give a creamy emulsion which when mixed with the pigment finish or season, it gives a waxy or non- tacky touch.

2. MONTAN WAX-

Melting Point = 76 to 84 degree c, It is obtained from shale oil. It is not a true wax but has properties similar to the paraffin wax, though it is usually darker- colored and has a higher melting point.

2- **CERESINE WAX-** Melting point = 60 to 85 degree c

It has a paler color, resembling bee wax and is obtained by distillation of ozokerite. All these waxes are known as saturated hydrocarbons and they are unsaponifiable.

3- **CARNUABA WAX-** Melting Point = 78 to 81 degree c

Carnauba wax is a yellow, brittle material of high melting point, extracted from the leaves of the Brazilian Palm. It may be purified by melting, filtering and bleaching to give more uniform (component) substance and a paler color. It is an expensive component of leather polishes, taking (producing) a high shine which is durable means not easily finger marked and to which dust and dirt do not easily deposit on the surface. These properties are due to its hard nature and high melting point. It can be emulsifying to give quality shoe cream, or such emulsion may be incorporated with leather finishes to give a waxy feel. It has smooth, non-tacky and good plating or polishing properties.

4- **BEE WAX-** Melting Point = 60 to 63 degree c It is obtained by melting the honey combs of bees after the removal of the honey. Color and quality vary and bleaching may be carried out to produce a palar, more uniform color. Its melting point is lower than that of carnauba wax and consequently it polishes more easily, but the shine is less durable and the surface remains somewhat tacky and liable to collect dirt. Good shoe polishes are usually a blend of the two, but the commoner types are based on cheap paraffin wax, hardened with the little carnauba wax or hard stearine. These may be made workable or softer by mixing with a proportion of turpentine or white spirit or may be emulsified with water to give shoe cream.

5- **SYNTHETIC WAX-**

There are a wide range of chemical products on the market classed as waxes, because of their physical properties. They may be synthesized to give a wide range of properties to required specifications.

Waxes are usually emulsified in water and stock solutions usually contain 10 – 15% solid wax. A traditional emulsifying agent is soap, which losses it's wetting power in contact with acid leather. Anionic or non- ionic surfactants are also used 5 – 10% of solid wax on the weight of solid binder is common. This will give a slight waxy feel, reduce the tackiness and sticking to hot glazing jacks and act as a release agent on hot plating or embossing. As the wax has to be wetted to emulsify it, it may give no improvement in water resistance and it may increase the wet-ability of the whole finish. Traditional waxes are carnauba and paraffin wax but many new synthetic waxes are available.

Impregnation of grain surface of the leather-

In finishing, it is necessary to fill the grain surface of the leather by surface impregnation which improves the quality of the finished leather. Surface impregnation is mostly done on corrected grain leather and is applied by seasoning pad, air- less spray or seasoning machine. The impregnating agent penetrate in grain layer, tighten it, in addition to offering the following advantages to the subsequent finish coats. The advantages are as follows-

1- Due to presence of the impregnating agent in the grain layer there is a partial penetration of the base coat thus giving better coverage.
2- The finishing coat is nicely anchored to the grain when plated
3- The grain break becomes smooth and fine.

Surface impregnants are of two types, namely –

a) Solvent based
b) Water based

a) SOLVENT BASED- Solvent based impregnate are usually pre-condensed polyurethane resins which penetrate the grain surface and react with the moisture and the active chemical groups in the leather.

b) Water based- Impregnate are much simpler to use and less hazardous water based. Impregnates are premixed with penetrations and require simple dilution with water.

SEASONS-

In many case, a transparent film or coating may be applied which modifies the shine, handle or fastness properties but leave the natural appearance of the leather visible- the so called aniline look. Such finishes are often referred to as seasons.

Traditionally these were the viscous solutions of water soluble colloids, ranging from proteins such as casein, egg- white albumin, gelatin and blood albumin to starch such as dextrin etc. Most of these products were form natural sources, liable to putrefaction and of non- uniform quality.

COMMON SEASONING AND THEIR PROPERTIES-

MATERIAL	CONCENTRATION	SPECIAL MERITS
1-Casein	1- 2% in alkaline soln.	Good gloss, good grain filling
2-Egg- albumin	1% in cold water	Very Good gloss
3-Linseed mucilage	2% digest in hot water	Dull gloss, soft feel
4-Cellulose Ether	½% in water	Dull gloss, good grain property.

There are many others and most of them can be mixed together to obtain the advantage of each constituent. A season originally consisted of water soluble of the above colloidal materials which on water evaporation, give the film. However, the season becomes modified by the addition of non-film forming dyes, waxes, oils and pigments. In these cases the colloid material not only formed a film but bound or stuck the additive to the leather surface and such materials are known as binders.

Apart from the above materials, some more sophisticated products are often used as seasons. Many of these are based on non- water systems and the mechanism of their film formation is different from water based systems.

OTHER SEASONS AND THEIR SPECIAL MERITS-

MATERIALS	CONCENTRATION	SPECIAL MERITS
1. Nitro- cellulose gloss Lacquer	Dilute 50/50 with water	water resistance, good
2-Vinyl resin flexibility & stretch	solvents	Very good in
3-Polyurethanes look	solvents	High gloss and wet
4-Polyuretane + water	Dilute in water & flexibility	Better absorption,
5-PU & NC dispersion characteristics.	Dilute in water	Better handle

Where season is diluted with solvent, there is no hydration of the leather fibers. Care must be taken if they are applied on top of a water based bottom coat to ensure that they have good anchorage and resistance to peeling.

LEATHER TYPE BRIEF DESCRIPTION- FINISHING

The current fashion trend in leather manufacture favors leather finished with **aniline look or semi- aniline look.** Leather finish with very little or no pigment in the finish coat. The idea of aniline or semi aniline look of leather is to give emphasis to the characteristics of natural leather, distinguishing it from the synthetics.

Finishing is divided into three parts-

1- Aniline Finish

2- Semi- Aniline Finish

3- Resin Finish

1- ANILINE FINISH-

This type of finishing is generally used in better quality of leather like glace kid leather, Glace kid cow softy, and shoe Nappa leather. In this finishing we use only dye- solution in season.

Aniline also called natural leather. This leather has the surface colored with transparent dyes. This transparency is similar to looking at the piece of stained wood. In fact, the grain stays natural and well visible. Aniline leather will have imperfections; it is nature's signature and assurance that every hide is one of a kind. These leathers have minimum surface protection thus more sensitive to the effect of use. Hence the leather that has not received any coating of pigmented finish. In another word- "the finish is completely transparent, so that the original grain surface can be seen through the finish completely unhindered by any pigment particles.

To make successful aniline leather some modifications in dyeing and finishing methods are necessary. The dyeing must be penetrative and level, bright and uniformly covered. The technique of dyeing is altered and adjusted by an intermediate treatment of cationic dye fixing agent with a view to producing a light pigmented effect during the dyeing process itself.

In the finishing of aniline leather the recent trend is the spray dyeing of leather surface with a dye solution in solvent as a base for producing aniline character.

To maintain this natural beauty it is mandatory to keep a routine of cleaning and protecting from the initial stage.

CHARACTERISTICS-

The aniline finish leather should have the following characteristics-

----- Look natural

----- Silky touch with good texture

----- Natural grain and marking

----- High comfort, breathable

For manufacturing of aniline leather the following points should be in mind-

1- We take only superior grade leather like 1st, 2nd and superior of 3rd.

2- Buffing is done on flesh side but no snuffing on grain side.

3- Impregnation is done on grain side to minimize the penetration of seasons.

4- Only dye solution is used as a coloring material no use of pigment.

5- As a binding material use only protein binder not resins binder because protein binder provides good gloss and attractive appearance.

6- Use egg- albumin to provide good and durable gloss.

7- Carnauba wax is generally used in this process because due to high melting point it form a thin film and provide good and durable gloss.

8- Small amount of penetrator and liquid ammonia are used for quick penetration in leather fiber and quick dry.

9- Aniline finish leather generally we prepared water proof with the season of formaldehyde and water.

SEMI- ANILINE FINISH-

Semi- aniline leather is defined as- Leather which has been aniline dyed or stained, incorporating a small quantity of pigment, not so much as to conceal the natural characteristics of the hide/ skin.

This type of finish is generally used in light snuffed leather. In this method we use the combination of dye solution and pigment.

This leather is covered with a lightly pigmented coat to make color uniform and hide minor defects. Transparent and brilliant colors are over sprayed to reconstruct the natural appearance of the leather. It has very light protection on it, so application of leather protector is recommended.

CHARACTERISTICS-

----- **Natural grain surface**

----- **Good look and feel**

----- **Improved light fastness**

----- **More practical than full aniline**

----- **Breathable**

Semi- aniline finishing is really a pigmented binder finish, but with restricted amounts of pigments and following the intension to have a restricted thickness of the total finish sheet with a aniline like look. It is the aim to produce semi- aniline leather because higher prices can be earned than with full pigmented leather. Many manipulations are made to obtain aniline like character of the surface. Two of them are bicolor effects and very slightly embossed artificial grain structure. If not embossed leather has to be finished in bicolor made the leather has to be dried by free hanging and should not be pressed, that the grain becomes "high". First the leather is finished with a lighter color and after pressing only the top of the grain structure are colored with a slightly darken color by spraying from a small angle side. Many other ways exist to obtain visual impressions of an aniline character. One of them is colorless final coat, or a coat colored only slightly with solvent dissolved organic dyestuffs. The total thickness of the semi- aniline finish is usually not greater than 20 micrometer and the applied mass not more than 20 g/m2. Semi- aniline in character is also all the numerous casein finishes more or less pigmented and not glazed or polished. This type of leather are in some cases not full rub fast mainly in wet condition. The finish layer generally is not thick and the color protection is not complete. But the feel of this leather is much more natural, it is a casein feel, very often the pigmentation is made with inorganic pigments, which are more brilliant in shade.

For manufacturing of semi- aniline finish the following points should be in mind-

1- For manufacturing of semi- aniline finish we take superior of 3rd grade + 4th grade +5th grade crust leather.
2- As a coloring material we take dye solution and pigment both.
3- As a binding material we take protein and resin binder both. Protein binder binds the dye solution and resin binder bind the pigment.
4- In this process the impregnation is not compulsory.
5- In this process egg albumin and ox blood is not required because it produce less gloss as compared to aniline finished leather.
6- In this process we use lower quality of wax like bee wax or combination of bee and carnauba wax to minimize the costing.
7- Buffing is done on flesh side but a light snuffing is require on grain Sside to minimize the grain defects.
8- A small amount of penetrator is required in season to penetrate the season in leather fiber.
9- For quick dry and smooth production a small amount of liquid ammonia is required for quick dry.
10- It has a very light protection so application of leather protector is recommended.

RESIN FINISH OR PIGMENTED FINISH-

In this method we use 100% pigment. Generally tanner's use this process because using pigment all the grain defects may be filled.

Impregnation-

Ammonia Liquor	50 ml.
Penetrator	50 ml.
Water	900 ml.

	One litre

One pad coat on grain side, hang it in shade and dry. If necessary do mollissa and check even feel. If the crust material is down selection, give light hair cell plate as per requirement.

Sealing coat-

Pigment	**100 ml/ gm**
Resin binder	**150 " "**
Wax	**25 gm**
Penetrator	**20 gm.**
Ammonia liquor	**10 ml**
Water	**695 ml**

Make the season one litre and mix it well. After that filter the season with cotton cloth and apply one pad coat on grain side. Dry it well.

Season coat-

Pigment	**100 parts**
Resin binder	**200 part**
Wax emulsion	**10 part**
Penetrator	**10 part**

Leather preservative (anti fungus) and small amount of Liquid ammonia also add.

Water	**660 part**

Make the season one litre. 2 to 3 spray coat for proper covering. Hang the material for proper dry. After that do top coat for proper gloss then final plate.

TOP COATS - ACQUOR AND THINNER-

Nitro- cellulose Lacquer = one part

Nitro- cellulose Thinner= two part

Mix well. One spray coat, dry, check shining. If necessary increase the pressure of spray gun. After one lacquer and thinner, the materials send to hydraulic press for proper plating.

This is the most widely used finishing technique and consists of a uniform surface by means of a base coat of pigments and resin followed with a protective top coat. They can be identified by their consistent color and uniformity. It is ideal for high use items like furniture or automotive seats, especially when you want your kids to use them "trouble- free".

CHARACTERISTICS-

------ **Consistent color**

------ **Improved light fastness**

------ **Good defect coverage and easy maintenance.**

TIPS FOR LEATHER FINISHING IDENTIFICATION-

The knowledge of identifying leather finish has been established to be a key aspect in the development of desired leather product. For any particular used, there are identifying some of the common leather finishes-

1- **DYE FINISH-**

Normally this type of finish is carried out for D. D. Lining, Nubuck and suede. Aniline finish also comes under this category. If dye are used with binder, known as **naked finish leather.**

2- **PROTEIN FINISH-**

Finish commonly used for grain leather, brittle in nature, dyes are main coloring material, poor water resistance, good gloss can be obtained.

3- GLAZED FINISH-

Conventionally it is a type of protein finish; the glazing effect is obtained by glazing machine. Compactness of grain is required to sustain the high temperature and pressure of the machine. Goat leather has been identified as the best material to produce glazed finish (Glace- kid). Some glazed leather is also available in the market with glazing appearance produced with different methodology.

4- RESIN FINISH-

Finish for corrected grain leather, prime constituent is acrylic or methacrylic binder, good covering power due to high content of pigments (coloring material with bigger particle size) , water resistance, Flexible & pliable in nature, cannot with stand very high temperature. Top coat is normally nitro- cellulose base lacquer and thinner.

5- SMOOTH FINISH-

This is a type of corrected grain finish, the closed defects are covered by repeating coating of season and pressing on hydraulic press, and finally plain plating is done to get smooth finished surface effect. Smooth C. G. leather can be glossy as well as dull in appearance.

6- PU FINISH-

Principal constituent is polyurethane binder. It can be further divided into PU Coated and PU Laminated and patent as per the processing techniques and final leather appearance. Waterproof surface can be obtained by PU finish.

7- PATENT FINISH-

Basically it is a PU finish in which a special type of curtain coater machine is utilized. The finish film thickness is restricted to be less than 0.15 mm. The mirror like appearance is the unique feature of this finish.

8- BURNISH-

Good burnishing effect can be observed using the specific tool, as in this case, a special type of wax is used in finishing season, giving dry & shiny surface effect after brushing. Usually burnish leather is dull looking grain leather before burnishing.

9- BRUSH- OFF-

This is also known as two- tone finish. After getting a uniform surface appearance of a particular color, final coating is carried out by spraying tinted lacquer of top coat color. This top color can be removed partially to get the brush- off effect during shoe making.

10- OIL -PULL -UP FINISH-

It can be carried out on Full Grain / Corrected Grain leather (snuffed). The pull-up oil (free oil) is well sprayed with the season and finally the oil is sealed inside by topcoat permitting the oil to move freely inside, responsible for color change when pulling the leather.

11- CRAZY – HORSE-

In this type of finish the wax content is more giving shade. The lower grade of crust is used for this and hence the snuffing is required more to hide the defects. The Crazy- Horse leather is developed without binder and the surface is found to be usually waxy. The color changes from dark to light when stretched.

12- NUBUCK/ SUEDE-

Nubuck is basically snuffed full grain leather with a fine velvety nap. Dye finish is carried out in this case without binder giving a good writing effect. On the other hand the suede is dye- finished on the flesh side of leather after buffing. The fiber-length is controlled during buffing so as to give the velvety touch to the surface. Split leather is also developed as suede, but lesser strength is found in split suede.

13- LAMINATED FINISH-

The lamination of the readymade finish film is carried out for obtaining this effect. The finish film can be of resin, PU etc. There are various techniques involved in film lamination. Basically this type of finish is advantageous for finishing split.

Types of leathers which may be encountered in finishing-

The current types of leathers which are encountered by the finishers may be subdivided as follows-

1- **CLASSICAL ANILINE LEATHER-** These are leathers of small area and of the topmost quality, with full grain, representing box and willow calf, glazed kid and other fine- grained leather. The leathers are drum dyed and finished with pigment free protein finishes for machine glazing.

2- **SLIGHTLY CORRECTED- GRAIN LEATHERS-** In contrast to fully corrected- grain, these leathers are only given a slight cover with finishes of low pigment content. They are lightly buffed to retain the fine pore structure of the grain and give a plating finish.

3- **BOX AND WILLOW SIDES-** This group comprises fairly heavy substance full-grained leathers with heavy retanning so that the feel of the leathers resemble that of semi- chrome leather. Here again a light cover is given with finishes of low pigment content.

4- **SEMI- ANILINE OR MOCK ANILINE LEATHERS-** These leathers with more or less heavy retanning are buffed and given a fairly heavy covering in the bottom coat. The finisher then uses his skill to give a slightly transparent darker tone on the top so that they look like aniline leathers. Sometimes the top seasons are adjusted with waxes, oils and solvents to give a pull up effect.

5- **CORRECTED GRAIN BOX AND WILLOW UPPERS- This** class represents the backbone of modern upper leather industry. The leathers which may be medium to heavily retanned may or may not have been drum dyed. These leathers require a plating finish with more or less heavy covering with pigment and resin dispersion binder. More deeply buffed leathers require a large quantity of binder than those which are lightly buffed.

6- **PRINTED LEATHERS WITH ANILINE- LOOK**- Leathers with grain blemishes (pox, ticks, blisters, vulture marks etc.) are covered with pigment finishes ande embossed with a variety of exotic grains. Subsequent top coat with an angular spray of darker tone emphasizes the aniline character by means of a two- color effect. These leathers must be heavily retanned so that the printing effect is deep and permanent.

7- **NORMAL GLAZED FINISH BOX AND WILLOW UPPER, LININGS AND COLORED KIDS ETC**- These are leathers of the medium quality full grain leathers which are drum dyed and finished with moderate quantity of pigment enriched with dyes to obtain brilliance in the finish. The leathers are machine glazed on protein finishes. In glazing finish, the gloss passes over the finished leather creating enough frictional heat to soften the film so that the finish film levels after glazing. The frictional heat generated may be 150 degree c or higher.

8- **GOAT GLAZED LEATHER**- Goat is the one of the best material for manufacturing of Glazed leather, because it has the fine texture and compact grain. For the manufacture of quality footwear we choose the material in wet blue stage. The selection should be only 1st and 2nd grade with even thickness in all portions. In this process we add the more syntans and less fat- liquors to avoid the looseness. In crust stage again we select the materials; if the flanks are loose then we cut the flanks because it is the more costly process of finishing. In finishing operation we do buffing on flesh side but no snuffing on grain side.

In finishing operation, we use-

Impregnation-

Dye solution	200 ml.
Protein binder	400 ml.
Water	400 ml.

Make the solution one liter. One spray coat, dry, plain plate- 80 degree c temperature and 120 bar pressure.

Season coat-

Dye- solution	100 ml.
Protein binder	150 ml.
Egg- albumin	15 ml.
Wax (carnauba)	10 ml.
Penetrator	10 ml.
Ox- blood	10 ml.
Liquid ammonia	10 ml.
Water	690 ml.

Make the season one liter. Mix well. Two to three light spray coat. Check covering. Dry well. Then send the material for glazing machine to provide proper glazing. If we required water proof glazed goat skin then apply-

Formaldehyde	200 parts
Water	800 parts

Make solution one liter. One spray coat, well dry. Then you provide the top coat for proper dressing.

POLYURETHANE EMULSION FOR LEATHER FINISHES

Polyurethane forms films that are flexible, tough and elastic. They when incorporated as binders in leather finishes give surface coatings having superior physical properties, such as abrasion, rub resistance, adhesion and flexibility over a wider temperature range than comparable polymers. Environment demands are making the use of solvents more difficult. Consumer requires leather having better and more consistent properties and although the world hides supply is slowly increasing and the surface is becoming worse. Finishers using polyurethane emulsions can help to solve these problems.

Initially available as solvent dilutable, there are now a wide range of water dilutable emulsions which can be used in environmentally friendly finishing systems to meet high performance demands from the consumer and which will upgrade leathers made from lower quality raw materials.

In this method, I will cover the following subjects.

1- The historical development of polyurethane.
2- The impact of environmental requirements.
3- Quality requirements.
4- Raw hides and skins availability and quality.
5- Properties of polyurethanes composed with other polymers.
6- The use of cross linking systems.
7- Leather substitutes.

HISTORICAL DEVELOPMENT-

The use of polyurethane has grown during the last 30 years. In the mind 1950 solve dilutable 2 components reactive PU polyurethanes comprising a di- isonate and polyol replaced the linseed oil process for making patent leather. The results were better flex, durability, appearance and ease of manufacture.

In 1959 a moisture cure reactive polymer for impregnating corrected grain leather was marked. The urethane was aromatic and solvent dilutable, the resultant impregnated leather had excellent scuff resistance, a very light breaks and improved cuttability.

About 1965, a new range of aliphatic urethane lacquers were introduced. They were still solvent dilutable but were fully reacted, had an infinite pot life and being an aliphatic isocyanate basis had excellent light fastness i.e. did not yellow. Being flexible they did not crack on ageing and offered a superior alternative to nitro- cellulose.

At the beginning of the 1970, the first water dilutable PU (polyurethane) emulsions were developed as adhesion promoters and sealers coats particularly for full grain leather on which conventional acrylic systems did not give the satisfactory result. The polymers were aromatic formed soft sticky films and the emulsions contained amounts of solvents.

An interesting reactive quick drying system solvent based for wet look and later water dilutable for conventional topcoats were developed in 1974. The principle was based on quick isocyanate system which becomes effective after solvent evaporation.

In 1977, a new family polyurethane emulsion binder was introduced for use of finishing splits. They were aliphatic i.e. light fast, fully reacted had no pot life, were true aqueous emulsions, contained only small amounts of coalescing solvents and were compatible with most auxiliaries e.g. other binders, fillers, pigments etc.

ENVIRONMENT ISSUES-

There has been a growing realization that our ways of living and manufacturing have damaged our environment. Stricter rules and regulations enforced by legislations are now a place to protect people and the environment both inside and outside the workplace. In many countries, stopping or restricting the use of solvents and ban on the use of certain chemicals. The reasons can be understood if one considers Arzinano in Italy, where there are approximately 300 tanneries producing 400 million square feet leather per year and where it is calculated that 30 tons per day of solvents are exhausted into the atmosphere each day.

VOC (Volatile Organic Compound) can not therefore be exhausted into the atmosphere, they can be recycled or burnt off, but this is impractical and expensive. The simple answer is to use solvent free finishes.

QUALITY REQUIREMENTS-

During the last few years there has been a growing requirement from the consumer driven especially by the automotive industry to meet specific and definite standards of product performance with regards to color, light fastness, abrasion and rub resistance and flexibility.

RAW MATERIAL-

Worldwide production of bovine hides, caprine, and ovine and pig skins is increasing annually on the average by in between 1 and 2% with most significant growth of bovine hides in developing countries with little or no growth in the OECD countries. Although there is some increase in supply to meet the extra demand, the quality standard is decreasing. Recently the demand for leather has been less particularly in the second half of 1990 and during 1991 because of the general world recession. The world economics improve pressure will be put back on the lower quality material.

PROPERTIES OF POLYURETHANES-

Urethanes polymers are produced by reacting polyisonates with poly functional alcohol. There are relatively few polyisocynates to draw from but a wide range of polyols for use and in practice it is the choice of the latter which is used to produce polymers with different end uses.

In order to produce urethane emulsions the cost of the raw materials and the more complicated production process results in more expensive products than conventional acrylics. The resultant properties of film produced have better elasticity and strength than other comparable types of binders. The two acrylics have lower tensile strength and elasticity compared to the urethane.

When actually used in finishes on leather other property improvement like adhesion cold crack and flex can be easily seen. The test results of a full grain leather finished with a simple resin and pigment base coat and top coated with lacquer emulsion show the effectiveness. They still need to be made into emulsions which have suitable flow and drying properties and which will give coherent films on the grain surface.

CROSS LINKING SYSTEMS-

In order to achieve higher levels of abrasions, flex and rub resistance required for high tech leathers cross linking or some from network is necessary to improve the film properties.

There are several cross linkers available, some highly effective, others are not so. One of the most effective is Polyaziridine, which gives excellent results on a variety of polymers but unfortunately from a toxicological point of view; it gives allergic reactions and has to be classed as toxic. It should be used only when handled carefully applying by precautions.

Another way of toughing a film is with an interpreting polymer network which is tougher and given reinforcement to a soft flexible film. Oligomers are used to produce such a network system. Compared against aziridines they are nontoxic but quite effective.

LEATHER SUBSTITUTES-

One of the most important long term developments affecting the leather industry and consequently the demand and price of leather is in field of leather substitutes. For centuries, leather has been considered the best material for boots and shoes as well as for many other articles due to the fact that it possesses a combination of qualities equaled by no known substitutes. The unique properties of leather are its capacity to breathe and to absorb sweat and water vapor which are essentially due to its fibrous structure and micro porosity. The collagen fiber bundles in the hides/ skins are woven into an intricate three dimensional tangle and are rendered in putrescible by tanning and leather is too complex a natural material to be amenable to synthesis by available technique. Advances in the field of high polymer technology have enabled the production of leather substitute and they have successfully replaced leather goods for various end uses. Approximately 65% of fancy leathers and footwear leathers have been substituted by synthetics.

Two types of synthetic leather are distinguishable-

- Products which resemble leather only in appearance, grain, nap, feel, and finish etc. but lack its intrinsic characteristics. These are cheap and attractive but are not real substitutes of the leather in the real sense. The face side of the plastic coated fabric products is embossed to produce the grain and surface finish of leather. The fabric is not fibrous and non-porous.
- The other class of synthetic not only looks like leather but also has its fibrous structure and micro porosity and possess some or all of its intrinsic properties through imperfectly. This leather like products are perspective, the real competitors or natural leather and the leather industry must watch the advances in this field. Sophisticated types of bonded and nonwoven fabrics, sheet materials made of tangled mats of natural or synthetic fibers belong to this class.

Restricted supplies and increased prices of leather may hasten the development and use of substitutes for leather in the importing countries. Substitutes are not likely to reduce materially the use of leather in the immediate future but rather to supplement it.

LEATHER TESTING-

The leather to be used for a particular construction must be tested to see if it has the properties needed. Note that the variability of leather places some constraints on testing. Leather is a natural material made from hides that vary in thickness and structure at different parts of the body. It is therefore not uniform but varies in its physical properties.

Tanned leather therefore varies within a hide and also between hides. It can be made surprisingly uniform during tannery processing. Enough is know about area variation for us into make definite conclusion from test results, provided the test are carried out on leather sampled from a standard position on the hide. Leather testing should be done in accordance with a recognized sampling procedure.

In general, the quality of leather is better assessed by sampling and testing from two or three different hides rather than from random pieces taken from the same hide. Testing should also take directional effects into account.

Another important variability in leather is that some of its physical properties vary with its moisture content. Moisture content is related to the relative humidity of the atmosphere in which the leather is stored. Accordingly, before leather is tested in a laboratory, it is conditioned for 48 hours under standard conditions of 20 degree c and 65% relative humidity (RH). Such conditions can be reproduced on a small scale for laboratory testing.

To evaluate the suitability of leather, the test results have to be compared against a known standard. In this section we use standards drawn guidelines for leather performance. These are only guidelines, and so each company may have to set different standards for its own requirements. Where standards are not available in the guidelines, we will give the expected level of performance.

PHYSICAL TEST-

The following tests are related mainly to the stresses which the upper leather encounters during manufacture, although some are encountered during wear. The two main tests are simple practical tests carried out in many shoe factories.

The first test assesses the tendency of leather to exhibit grain cracking or bursting during lasting. One method of testing for cracking is the key test, where a key or other smooth rounded object is pushed into the leather to distend it from the flesh side and then drawn firmly across the leather. This test, which can be done in the factory, is particularly useful when finish grinning is likely to occur.

In the second test, to assess the leathers resistance to tearing, the footwear manufacturer cuts a slit in the edge of the skin and then continues tearing it by hand to assess the leather resistance to tearing. Both these tests are, of course, not very accurate, and so more consistent and scientific tests have been developed to replace them.

Grain strength is usually assessed using a lastometer, which operates on a simple principle. A 25 mm diameter leather disc is clamped into the lastometer, and a 6 mm diameter steel ball, on the end of a steel rod, is forced into the flesh side of the leather, until the grain cracks or less often, the leather bursts. The force exterted against the leather at grain crack and the extension of the leather at that point can both be measured. The lastometer thus measures the tendency of an upper leather to crack or tear in lasting end give information about its strength and degree of extensibility under multidirectional strain.

Tear strength- When leather is hand- torn in the factory the resistance to tearing is only estimated, but at LASRA, a machine is used to measure this resistance. The standard tear- strength test uses a specially designed test piece, and the load to start the tear is measured using a tensile tester.

Specially designed hook- type jaws are used to fit into the center slot of the sample. The jaws are attached to a tensile tester, and the load needed to tear the sample is measured.

A tensile tester measures the strength and stretch of materials. It can be a relatively simple device or a complex highly accurate instrument. The tear strength of any particular leather depends on its type and thickness. Tear strength determines the uses to which the leather is put and the degree of reinforcement that has to be provided.

Calf, and lining leathers (0.7 mm)	40 N
Side leather (1.0 – 1.2 mm)	40 N
Side leather (1.3 – 1.5 mm)	80 N
Side leather (above 1.5 mm)	120 N

Tensile strength-This is the load necessary to break a piece of leather of known width and thickness. Although it is a good measure of intrinsic leather quality, it is not as easily related to shoemaking requirements as is a lastometer or a tear- strength tests. The tensile test can be used to measure the load at certain percentage extensions, which can indicate the foot- comfort properties of leather. For example- a leather with a low load at 5% extension is soft and stretches easily, thus exerting less stress on the foot.

CHEMICAL TESTS

The chemical properties of a leather depends on the tanning processes. In footwear manufacturer, we are concerned three chemical properties-

CHROME CONTENT- The heat resistance of chrome- tanned leather depends partly on their chrome content. A minimum chrome content of 4% has been suggested for leather to be used in vulcanised footwear. However, the more moisture content of the leather at vulcanizing is probably more important. The analyses of chrome content requires considerable expertise and is best carried out by the tanner or an independent laboratory.

A simplified test to assess the heat resistance of chrome leathers can be used in the footwear factory. A strip of wet leather is immersed in boiling water for 2 minutes. If the shrinkage is greater than 5%, the leather probably is unsuitable for vulcanized footwear.

FAT CONTENT-

After tanning, oils and fats are determined into the leather to make it softer, fuller, more flexible, and sometimes to increase its water proofness. Fats and oils can migrate into sole- bonding, adhesives and react with the heat stabilizers to form soaps, which can contaminate the surface and reduce adhesion. Neoprene adhesives are more sensitive to such contamination than polyurethane adhesives. Obviously, the greater the fat content, the greater the likelihood of contamination.

The following maximum fat contents have been set down the guidelines for the various adhesives.

7% for direct vulcanizing

9% for one- component adhesives

14% for two- component adhesives

Fat content is measured by extracting the fat from the leather with a suitable solvent, usually dichloromethane. It is not a test easily carried out in the footwear factory.

MINERAL- SALT CONTENT- When leather components have an excessive salt content, while salt spues may appear on the upper. The mineral- salt content is called the **sulphated Ash of water soluble (SAWS).** High SAWS contents usually result from inadequate washing-out of the leather during tannery processing, and the following maximum guidelines are applied.

Upper leather (except patent)	0.8%
Lining leather	1.0%

FINISH TEST

The appearance of the shoe may be spoilt by the loss of finish by its cracking. The wearer's feet may be stained by color, usually from lining leathers and the inside of unlined uppers. Poor resistance of the finish or color to rubbing can cause both marring and transfer, but marring can also be caused by poor adhesion of the finish or poor resistance to flexing.

Three tests are commonly used to define the performance of a leather finish-

FINISHED ADHESION- In this test, the finish side of the leather is bonded to a brass plate with an adhesive, usually Araldite that does not soften or affect the finish. The test assembly is left for the adhesive to cure, and then the leather is peeled away from the plate. Because the finish adheres more strongly to the plate than to the leather. It is left behind on the plate, and the load needed to remove the finish can therefore be measured.

The standard of performance depends on the thickness of the finish film, the thicker the film- the greater the adhesion required and whether the leather has been dyed to a matching color. The following minimum values have been found to be realistic-

Corrected- grain (pigment) finishes	dyed	400 N/ m
	Undyed	500 N/m
Full grain finishes		250 N/m
Patent (polyurethane) finishes		500 N/ m

In addition to this precise adhesion test, a useful check is to stick firmly on to the finish a strip of pressure- sensitive tape and then peel it off slowly. The surface finish may have to be cut through to start the separation. If much of the finish comes off with the tape, the adhesion is not good enough. Although sellotape has been widely used, more consistent pressure- sensitive tapes are available. This test provides a quick method of assessing the adhesion of the finish. If failure occurs, it should be brought to the attention of the tanner.

FLEX RESISTANCE-

The breakdown of uppers in wear occurs mainly in the vamp region, due to the continualflexing of the upper in that area. Thus, one of the best tests of wearing quality is a flexing test. We have said that leather, unless affected by perspiration or wetting rarely breaks down through flexing and that the finish usually fails first.

Many ordinary leather finishes develop a fine cracking or crazing in wear over all the upper except the toe- cap and stiffener regions. This marking does not seem to be a cause of complaint, unless it cannot be covered by shoe polish or the finish flakes, but with patent or wet- look finishes, flex cracking of the finish is very obvious and is a definite cause of complaint.

A test is therefore required to simulate the flexing action that occurs in wear. The most common flexing machine for testing leathers is the **Bally Flexometer,** developed by Bally Footwear Manufacturers in Switzerland. In which the leather is flexed in a folded position so that the test specimen undergoes a rolling motion.

If a leather finish has poor resistance to flexing, this test quickly shows it up. A satisfactory finish should withstand 10,000 flexes without showing significant cracking, that is, cracking that could not be covered by polish.

The finish of patent leathers, which is more prone to flex cracking failure, is further required to show no cracking after 1,000 flexes when the leather is wetted. This test simulates the build- up of perspiration in the leather. Because the finish is almost impermeable, continued exposure to moisture can reduce the adhesion of the polyurethane finish to the leather.

Although the flexing action of the Bally does not simulate the flexing that occures in the vamp of the shoe with the accuracy of the SATRA upper-material flexing machine. It remains the preferred way to test the flex resistance of all leathers. We will examine the role of the SATRA flexing machine when looking at synthetic upper materials.

RUBFASTNESS-

The loss of finish due to light scuffing and rubbing, and the transfer of color to hose and trouser cuffs can be checked using a rubfastness test.

A common test in the factory is to rub the finish with a moistened white cloth to see if the cloth is quickly discolored by the finish. Like many factory tests, it is very dependent on personal assessment. To the more meaningful, a rubfastness test should use a standard rubbing medium, a standard pressure, length of rubbing time, and method of assessment.

A circular felt pad, which can be dry or wet, does the rubbing, revolving under a standard load on the leather finish for a specified period. The marring of the leather finish and the transfer of color to the felt pad can both be assessed against what are called the **Standard Grey Scales.**

One Grey Scale is for marring and one for transfer. Each scale is divided into five graduations. For transfer, the Grey scale goes from white through shades of grey to black. The scale for marring goes from black through grey to white. From these scales, the degree of greyness that most nearly matches the discoloration is measured on the 1- 5 scale. The higher the rating, the better the rubfastness.

For full grain and corrected- grain finishes, a minimum requirement is set of Grade 3 for transfer and marring after 128 wet rubs. For the grain surface of hide suedes and for lining leathers, a higher requirement is set of Grade 4 for transfer after 128 wet rubs.

The rubfastness tester, which is simple and quick to operate, should be used in shoe factory. However, shoe-room dressings can significantly affect the performance of the finish. In many cases of complaint, the shoe room dressing has failed, not the tannery finish. Rubfastness and adhesion tests can therefore be used to assess the performance of various dressings on the leathers being used. Lining leathers, particularly quarter linings, are also continually rubbed by stockings. The Martindale Abrasion test, in which the abrasive is a woolen fabric, provides test conditions of the right severity. A disc of leather is clamped in a holder and rubbed against a base covered with the woolen fabric. The leather sample travels over the whole area of the square of fabric in predetermined patterns.

This test can wear many sheepskins in to a hole in a reasonable test time and partly remove the grain of goat leathers, as happens during the wearing of the shoe. Calf and kid leathers are largely untouched, and suede has the nap removed and is then polished. No definite standards of performance have been set for the Martindale abrasion resistance of leathers because, although it can detect broad differences, it is not known to pick out smaller differences between leathers of the same type.

MISCELLANEOUS TESTS-

The following are some of the many tests that can be used to determine many of the other properties of leather.

WATERPROOFNESS-

When this property of leather was examined at SATRA it was noted that few complaints were made about the performance of leather in everyday footwear. In some specialist areas, leather is expected to have a higher level of water resistance, and so a test is needed to measure the relative performance of leathers. For this test we generally use Bally Penetrometer.

This equipment determines the water resistance of upper leathers under simulated conditions. The test samples are weighed and then flexed while partially submerged in water. The time for penetration of water, shown by the indicator lights, is recorded. After penetration, the test is continued for a complete hour from penetration and then the sample is re-weighed. The increase in weight shows the amount of water absorbs.

The water transmission is subsequently determined during further hours of flexing time by measuring the water absorbed by a cloth wick placed in the sample. Thus, the test measures water penetration time, water absorption, and water transmission. The permanency of water resistance can be determined by drying out the test samples and repeating the test a number of times. Each subsequent test on a particular sample can normally be expected to give poorer results.

The degree of water proofness required of upper leather depends on what it is to be used for. However, the following Ministry of Defence Specification for boot upper leathers provides a guide-

Water penetration time	minimum 30 minutes
Water absorption	maximum 20%
Water transmission	maximum 0.5 g in first hour after penetration.

BREAK-

The appearance of leather in wear must also be considered. We require that a leather shall be not so loose-grained or pipey as to give a poor appearance to the upper. Note that pipey leather is not necessarily weak and usually withstands manufacture and wear.

This feature is commonly tested by folding a depression in the leather with the thumb or forefinger and noting the degree of wrinkling.

Attempts have been made to provide a quantitative standard for the judgement of break, the most recent and successful being the SATRA Break/ pipiness Scale.

In this test, a sample piece of leather or the vamp is placed grain side up around a special mandrel. The appearance of the break of the sample is then compared with the break scale, which has 8 images of similarly folded samples. This numbered scale permits a more objective evaluation of leather break.

We have examined the range and usefulness of leather testing, but remember that existing test procedures probably do not reproduce all the types of abrasion or scuffing damage that occur in wear. Testing cannot and less not claim to predict all problems and failures, but it can prevent many of the more serious failures. The fact that many companies continue to carry out regular testing shows its usefulness.

QUALITY REQUIREMENT FOR FINISHED LEATHER

Depending on the end- use and type of leather, a wide spectrum of quality based on visual, physical, chemical and instrumental techniques have to be carried out in a workshop. With leather being a non-homogeneous commodity, performance tests have an important role to play in assessing its quality.

To obtain a standard leather of required quality for a specific end use it is necessary to use selected raw materials, chemicals and leather auxiliaries.

To maintain high quality standards in leather, it is necessary that the quality of raw stock as well as auxiliaries such as general purpose chemicals like sodium sulfide, lime powder, sulfuric acid etc. agents like vegetable and chrome tanning extracts and performance chemicals including syntans, dyes, fat- liquors and finishing chemicals should be tested periodically for their quality.

Recently there has been a growing awareness among the public regarding the quality of customer goods and this is coupled with international systems such as ISO- 9000/ 14000 and Environmental and Pollution Control aspects.

This is possible only when the concepts of proper testing for quality are introduced in the raw materials and chemical inputs in processing industries such as tanning.

Hence, an effective physical and chemical testing laboratory and technical services center for quality control, developing suitable recipes and carrying out practical evaluation and performance trials is essential in the modern competitive environment.

The ultimate aim is to introduce high quality innovative eco- friendly and cost effective concepts into the leather industry. The establishment of such a center for a cluster of tanneries in a region can solve the day- to-day production and process problems to maintain quality standards of their products.

TECHNICAL ASPECTS-

The most important factor influencing the physical properties of leather is the fiber structure. Physical properties are determined as per standards method under specified temperature and relative humidity. Prior to testing, the samples have to be conditioned in a standard atmosphere; this can be best achieved by the installation of air conditioning equipment in the physical testing lab.

The ultimate quality test for leather is to assess its performance in wear or use under natural conditions in a wear trial. To reduce the planning and cost involved in such trials, laboratory machines are used to simulate natural conditions such as flexing and water penetration in addition to the various physical characteristics of leather.

A combination of two or more properties has to be tested to ensure the quality of the leather for a particular use. For example- Sole leather has to be tested for water absorption as well as resistance to abrasion, upper leathers for flexural endurance, fastness to rubbing, water vapor permeability etc.

CHEMICAL TESTING-

The main object of chemical testing is to provide assistance to the leather industry in the quantitative and qualitative analysis of eco- sensitive chemicals present in leather products as well as their chemicals used in the processing.

In view of the importance of leather as an export commodity and the recent ban on several of the chemicals by importing countries, it has become necessary to establish modern facilities to analyze such chemicals. There are a number of banned azo dyes, because the cleavage of one or more azo bonds, they could form any of the twenty aromatic amines. Azo dyes are most important chemical in the class of dyes, representing 60 – 70% of all dyes used. However, their use in banned in the manufacture (in Germany) of regulated consumer goods and their presence in detectable amounts in regulated products placed on the German market. The presence of these banned aryl amines have to be analyzed.

PENTACHLOROPHENOL-

Pentachlorophenol (PCP) is sometimes used as preservative and as an anti- mould agent in leather processing, so it is obviously harmful to living organisms. The German regulation specifies a maximum limit of 5 mg/ kg, which in practice means a ban on the use of PCP.

The presence of Cr (VI) in the final leather may occur due to the presence of Cr (VI) in pigments, un-reduced Cr (VI) during the preparation of basic chromium sulfate or the oxidation atmosphere in leather processing and subsequent period. The Cr (VI) present in the leather is reached out from the leather and then measured calorimetrically using a spectrophotometer after making complex coloration with diphenyicarbazide.

GENERAL CHEMICALS-

The general chemicals such as wetting agents, lime powder, sodium sulfide, ammonium chloride, sodium chloride, sulfuric acid, formic acid and borax etc. have to be analyzed for their purity.

CHECKING OF TANNING AGENTS-

Tanning agents employed in leather processing, such as wattle extract and myrobalan extract, have to be analyzed for their tannin/ non tannin content and mineral tanning agents such as basic chromium sulfate and aluminium tanning salts, have to be analyzed for their Cr_2O_3 and Al_2O_3 content respectively.

Based on the field survey and also keeping in mind the quality control of leather, it is important that the majority of the chemical tests set out in the SLTC official methods are carried out.

MICROSCOPICAL AND BACTERIOLOGICAL TESTS-

This is a technique used as a quality control tool on raw skins; semi processed pelts or finished leather. The opening up and the orientation of the fiber structure of skins during the different processes of tanning operations can well be assessed by microscopic examination.

If the curing is improper or insufficient then there is every possibility of bacterial damage. The extent of damage of the skin can be judged by viewing a cut section under the microscope. In addition, it is an effective tool to determine the presence of stains, defects, discoloration etc. in the leather.

During storage, wet blue or E. I. Leathers, finished leathers, leather goods and vegetable tan liquors are sometimes attacked by moulds, which can easily be detected by the microscopic examination.

The bacteriological tests are also quite important. The bacterial population associated with a fresh salted skin will provide preliminary indications about the quality.

These examinations help in determining the resistance of skin/ leather for bacterial/ fungal growth, and also help to find out efficiency of various bactericide/ fungicide used in preserving the leather.

PROCESS / PRODUCT DEVELOPMENT LAB-

The basic objective of the process/ product development laboratory are – development of sample leather as per control samples supplied by the buyers, the re- standardization of the process parameters for material/ energy optimization, the development of alternative techniques of manufacturer in situations arising out of changes in raw materials and chemical qualities and the introduction of new

The facility may include sample drums, specifically suited for dyeing, processing skins and hides. The sample drum should have facilities such as proper rpm, temperature and time for better process control. This facility can cater to the needs of tanners interested in performing sample experiments with a small number of pieces.

The process control facilities consists of an automatic chemical weighing system with a load cell, hot water still and specially designed working platform for charging and drum operating / monitoring. After automatically weighing, the chemicals are transferred by gravity into a receiver on a trolley, which is equipped with a transfer pump and necessary piping.

It can be moved nearer to the drum for charging. The liquid effluent streams from the experimental drums are let out of the process/ product development lab through the appropriately designed drain system. A separate store room is recommended for safety considerations.

COLOR MATCHING AND CAD/ CAM-

The facility could be used to serve the industry with computer aided color matching of dyed leather samples, so it should be equipped with spectrophotometer capable of measuring L*, a*, b*, c* and h values. A CAD facility can help industries by creating computer- aided design for footwear or leather goods.

OTHER POINTS-

Analysis of effluent liquor such as for BOD, COD and TDS etc. will need to be carried out and will analysis of process water such as for hardness.

For health and safety, it is recommended that adequate ventilation is provided in

the building. All electrical installation should be properly grounded, and normal fire fighting facilities should be adequate for the storage area for chemicals and other areas. It is also recommended to take proper personnel protective measures wherever needed. Safety and fire fighting equipments identified for the centre.

CONCLUSION

The production of uniform quality leather depends upon the proper selection of raw materials, chemicals, auxiliaries, formulation and judicious adjustments and manipulations in the manufacturing process and finishing operations by developing suitable recipes.

The testing lab and technical service for tanneries and product units is essential for working out newer techniques to improve quality, upgrading low grade leather to realize higher unit value, to work out chemical and water saving in order to reduce pollution load without sacrificing the quality.

Hence effective physical and chemical tests and technical service center for quality control, developing suitable recipes and carry out practical evaluation and performance trials is essential in the modern competitive environment in which rapid and sustained introduction of high quality, innovative, eco- friendly and cost effective leather/ leather products have become the order of the day.

SHOE - FINISHING

Shoe making is a rough process. Most of the operations during its manufacture are meant for giving it a proper shape. During process, the upper material is subjected to a wide variety of abrasive and stretching operations, which can adversely affect its appearance and sometimes even in heart its characteristics.

Hence good shoe finishing will enhance the image of our enterprise and product brand image. This image can be influence by the overall looks and appearance, which in turn is affected by the following, all of which are achieved by finishing work.

1- Degree of brightness
2- Feel (waxy finish etc.)
3- Special effects- like shadowing, antiquing.
4- Cleaning- lack of marks and flaws
5- Durability of the finish during in wear.

Water resistance of the shoe upper can also be enhanced by a suitable finish.

COMMON MATERIALS USED IN SHOE MAKING-

Materials used for shoe making from shoe finishing point of view are mentioned as-

UPPER MATERIAL- Leather, synthetic, fabric etc.

BOTTOM MATERIAL- Sole, insole, heel etc.

The end purpose of shoe finishing is to add value for the customer, by improving the aesthetic. Actually the good finishing provides appeal to the shoes and develops brand loyalty. Actually finishing provides the value addition of the final product. Lastly we say that finishing can significantly improve customers interest in the product, and consequently to higher returns.

FUNCTION OF LEATHER/ SHOE FINISH-

The functions of shoe finishing are as follows-

1- To produce a standardized color and appearance.
2- To produce a uniform degree of gloss.
3- To protect the leather against adverse chemical & physical influence.
4- To produce a surface that can be suitably cleaned by the ultimate user.

GROUPING OF LEATHER TYPES FOR FINISHING PURPOSES-

Generally, three finishing layers are given at the tannery.

1- Ground Layer
2- Intermediate Layer
3- Top Layer

GROUND LAYER- The ground layer is given to prepare the surface for successive coats and to provide adhesion between the leather and the other layers. It is the first application of seasons in grain leather.

INTERMEDIATE LAYER- The intermediate layer prevents the major portion of the leather thickness. By the use of intermediate layer we generally hide the grain defects which are visible on grain surface.

TOP COAT / TOP LAYER- The top layer provides the gloss and protects the leather from damages. It also gives the leather the feel and aesthetic appeal. From the shoe finishing point of view, the top layer given at the tannery is crucial.

TYPES OF LEATHER-

1- **ANILINE FINISH LEATHER-** Color transparency and brightness. Soft pliable leather tanned from the young animals. Used for good quality fashion shoes for men and women. Characterized by a soft grained and glossy appearance. Aniline leather is most natural looking leather with the unique surface characteristics of the hide/ skins grain visible. Aniline leather is colored only with dye and not with a surface coating of polymer and pigment. A light surface coating may be applied to enhance its appearance and after slight protection against spillages and soiling.

2- **PIGMENTED LEATHER**- Appearing both under full grain & corrected grain leather, is covered with pigments and required strong cotton brush zxx1application. Pigmented leather is the most durable but is less natural in appearance, having a polymer coating. Pigmented leather is a leather whose surface has a finish containing pigment particles that render the finish completely opaque. This leather is used in the majority of furniture upholstery and almost all car upholstery. The durability is provided by a polymer surface coating which contains pigments. The surface coating allows the manufacture more control over the properties of leather, resistance to scuffing or fading. The thickness of the surface coating can vary.

3- **NAPPA LEATHER**- Its main quality is soft and silky touch with round feel and needs to be finished in a delicate manner. A high quality of wax is generally used in operation to provide silky texture on the surface of the leather because most of the nappa leather is used in garments manufacturing.

4- **BURNISH LEATHER**- It is vegetable tanned or chrome tanned leather. Its top layer is treated with special wax which gives it a burnishing effect on burnishing. A high abrasive action by a rotary cotton roller is required for this type. Generally after waxing it provides two tone effects on the surface of the finished shoes. This finish is normally given on full grain leather.

Good burnishing effect can be observed using the specific tool as in this case a type of burnishing wax is used during finishing giving dry & shiny surface effect. When you burnish something, you are making the object shiny using friction and pressure. Leather is usually burnished at the edges, such as on a belt, using a metal tool like a spinning disk. Burnishing is different than polishing as no polish is used in the process. Leather must be fairy moist when burnishing, but no wet.

5- **BRUSH OFF LEATHER-** It is thick leather generally finished with heavy finish base on which a removable product either in contrast color or darken in shade than the base is applied. Once the leather is brushed, it becomes brilliant with a two tone effect.

6- **EMBOSSED LEATHER-** These are embossed in order to hide the defects or to create a particular appearance, such as reptile, zug-grain, fine hair cell, shrunken grain etc. Soft cutting brush is required for such leather and application of filler, as we shall see later should be avoided. A large proportion of the hide or skin coming to the tannery are full of defects and they are either unusable or it is very costly for shoe manufacturers to use them. The tanner therefore, endeavors to improve the quality by eliminating or rendering these defects by a procedure. The leather is buffed from the grain side and then finished, plated at high temperature and pressure to give it a good appearance and grain finish with heavy coats of pigmented finish. Since correction of grain pattern takes place in the whole process, to hide the defects and increase the cutting value, this leather is called corrected grain leather or Embossed leather. Based on different design and different plates, different names is given to this leather.

7- **NUBUCK & SUEDE LEATHER-** Nubuck provide a fine nap because of the tight fiber structure in the grain layer. It is used to manufacture a high quality of shoes. The dye finish is done on nubuck leather. This leather has got a very good writing effect. Writing effect is the effect caused to raised naps on the surface. When we apply our Finger on the surface we get ginger marks on this leather. This effect is called writing effect. Buff nubuck has low writing effect. This leather is usually aniline leather that has a sanded surface to give a fine, velvety surface, the look and feel of these leathers are incomparable and work well for low use applications. Its main characteristics is velvet look and touch, high comfort and breathable smooth touch. Where as the suede the flesh side of the leather buffed to produce a fine velvety nap, applied to calf, kid etc. The suede leather mostly produced from split leather. Dye finish is carried out in this case without binder and then proper fixation of the dye is done.

If the leather is made velvety from both sides, it is called split suede. Course fibers of similar look are visible from both the sides. This leather can be utilized from both the sides. If grain side is totally defective then the flesh side is made usable by giving it a velvety appearance. This leather is called **reverse side suede.**

8- **GLAZED LEATHER-** It is a type of leather in which a type of protein finish is done and the glazing effect is obtained by glazing machine. Glazed leather is a leather treated with a pigment containing not only gloss, but also protection. Compactness of grain is required to sustain the high temperature and pressure of the machine. Glazed finish is again a natural finish given normally on goat/ kid leather. This has a very brilliant and natural gloss.

9- **PATENT LEATHER-** Patent finish is basically a PU finish in which a special coating is carried out. The finish film thickness is restricted to be less than 0.15mm. The mirror like appearance is the unique features of this finish.

Patent PU coated or PU film coated is a split leather with a thick film of PU laminated on it. This leather does not have breakability like leather because of thick PU film. In earlier times before the mid of this century, it was an art to produce patent leather based on hardening of coatings from linseed oil drying on the air in the sun.

Only very few and therefore very famous factories could do that properly. In case of D. D. Lack, the brand names stand for a disocynate and polyester. On mixing both in appropriate relation and by a appropriate dilution viscous solution of 25 – 40% are prepared with a profile of some hours. Drying and hardening occurs in few hours. The grounded leather has to be coated very "wet" flat lying extended in frames. Patent leather has a high gloss and film thickness of until to 100 microns. PU film coated leather is either a split or sometimes full grain leather with a very thin film of PU laminated on it. This leather breathes.

10- **SOLE AND INSOLE LEATHER-** (Vegetable tanned) - Leather was always the main soling material. The leather which is used as soling material is vegetable tanned buff leather and varies thickness from 4 mm- 7 mm. Sole leather should be solid, bold. Flexible. It should not wear out easily, it must not increase in area as a result of shoe wearer's body pressure and at the same time it should not crack when subjected to a certain degree of blending on a specified metallic ball or rod.

The real secrecy of vegetable tanning of heavy leathers like the sole lies mainly with their degree of tannings, which can be defined as the quantity of vegetable tannins fixed by 100 gms of the hide substance. For high value of D. T. (Degree of tanning) a large quantity of tannins should enter into pelt and at the same time chemically react with collagen, so that the tannins can not be extracted out with water.

The degree of tanning of sole leather is highest and lies between 90 & 95, even though this degree of tanning for leather can be raised up to 120 or more. When D. T. exceeds 100 the fiber structure of leather gets disoriented or destroyed and the leather becomes hard like piece of horn which can not be made flexible with the best lubrication.

SHOE FINISHING PROCESS

A shoe finish is intended for rectifying certain material imbalances occurring during shoe fabrication. This is achieved by adopting three important stage process of using cleaners, fillers, repair and top coat.

There are various process involved in shoe upper finishing. The following are the main process.

1- Cleaning
2- Repairing
3- Wrinkle chasing
4- Filling by base coat application
5- Top Coat application
6- Dressing

1- CLEANING OF UPPER-

Before starting finishing of upper operation, ensure that the surface to finish has been totally clean. The main purpose of cleaning the upper of the shoes is-

----- **To remove the dirt, adhesive overspill, and other unwanted marks and contaminations.**

----- **To condition the finish surface to accept dressing and/ or other treatment.**

Cleaning can be done **before or after** removing the last from the shoe. The latter is preferable for better shape retention of the shoe.

When necessary, cleaning of lining is also done.

PRINCIPLES TO FOLLOW WHEN CLEANING- Three types of cleaners based on water, solvent water mixture and solvents are used depending upon the material,- leather or non- leather. Water based cleaners constitute soap, water and a wetting agent. Addition of ammonia enhances the cleaning effect. Water solvent cleaners contain in addition to water a solvent like methylated sprit. Solvent based cleaners contain one or more of petrol, petroleum spirit, alcohol or acetone. Solvent based cleaners are good for degreasing.

1- **Relate the choice of cleaner and the method of cleaning to the type of contamination that is being removed and the type of finish on the upper.**

For example—Solvent – based cleaners should be used to soften natural rubber, (because water based will not).

However, do not try to remove rubber solution from suede with a solvent – based cleaner or **"tide marks"** will result. Suede has to be cleaned dry by rubbing with crepe rubber.

2- **Use dry method in preference to wet.**

3- **Use the mildest treatment possible that will effectively remove the contamination.**

The stronger the cleaner, the more finish it will remove in cleaning.

Start with the mildest cleaner, and try progressively stronger cleaners until the dirt is removed.

TYPES OF LIQUID CLEANERS-

The types of cleaners can be divided into the following categories.

1- WATER BASED CLEANERS-

These are usually very mild types of cleaners, and contain soaps, wetting, dispersing and emulsifying agents (detergent), and sometimes weak alkalis such as ammonia dissolved or suspended in water.

Water based cleaners are mild enough to be used for machine cleaning and are suitable for overall removal of the general grime and dirt picked up in the factory from handling. Care should be taken with cleaners containing ammonia on some types of leather finish.

2- **WATER / SOLVENT BASED CLEANERS-**

Cleaners of this type are made from solvents that mix with water such as **methylated spirit and acetone.** Some of these can be very strong, and will quickly attack and strip off some finishes.

These cleaners are suitable for overall cleaning of certain finishes that are unaffected by these solvents such as PU coated fabrics, patents etc. They have a big advantage over water based, that they dry much quicker.

3- **SOLVENT BASED CLEANERS-**

The solvents in this type are usually derived from petroleum and can be mixed with other solvents of the same type to give different cleaning powers.

These are suitable for removing grease, oils and waxes, and the weaker blends can be used for overall cleaning of certain finishes. They are very quick in dry.

4- **CLEANERS / POLISHERS-**

Cleaners / polishers are supplied as gels and contain solvent cleaners and polishing agents, which remain on the surface after the solvents have evaporated.

Application is by sponge or cloth and after drying can be polished on a power mop.

These are very suitable for patents and PU coated fabrics, and have the advantage of giving an acceptable semi- bright finish without having to spray.

5- **CONDITIONERS-**

Conditioners open up the surface, softens the leather and acts as an adhesive binder between the leather and the finish. Conditioners are water based cleaners containing a high quality film forming resin which acts as a cross- linker. Conditioners are water based and are designed to open up the surface for efficient cleaning.

CLEANING METHODS-

Cleaning can be done both **"wet" & "dry" by hand and by machine.**

CLEANING DRY BY HAND-

The items used for this cleaning method are-

1- **Crepe rubber-** For removal of adhesives.

2- **Soft sponge rubber-** For brushing the suede nap.

3- **Brushes- Wire and stiff bristle type-** For removing general dust and dirt from suede and brushing up the suede nap.

4- **Scouring pads- For** removing general dust and dirt from suede.

5- **Dull knives- For** scraping away hard substances like waxes. Sometimes warming the knife slightly to get the knife under to lift contaminants from the surface.

6- **EMERY PAPER- Various fine grades of grit-** For raising and even up any suede nap that has been badly treated or discolored.

Cleaning dry also is the method on all types of fabrics, as liquids leave **"tide marks".** The best solution is to avoid getting the shoes dirty in the first place as heavy staining is impossible to remove.

CLEANING DRY BY MACHINE-

The machine can have power driven, revolving brushes of various shapes. The method requires that the upper finish of material will stand up to friction and the heat generated by brush. Apply just sufficient pressure to remove dirt without damaging the finish. Usually, removing some stubborn contaminations by hand methods is necessary. The machine has an applicator for cleaner and usually a mild water- based type is chosen for general cleaning.

(a)- Adjust the amount of cleaner applied to revolving brush to wet out the material without being excessive.

(b)- take care not to over brush and damage the finish.

(c)- Follow the work method-

1- Clean the feather area with the small wet cleaning brush.

2- Clean the upper with bigger wet brush.

3- Dry the upper with the bigger wet brush.

4- Polish on the woolen brush.

CLEANING WET BY HAND-

Advantages of hand cleaning is that selective cleaners can be used, and an operative can give to each shoe individual treatment.

1- Apply the cleaner by cloth (white cotton piece are best) wrapped round the finger by rubbing gently over the surface. Or by sponge when very little rubbing pressure is required. Stubborn dirt may need extra rubbing or application of a more suitable cleaner.

Crepe rubber and dull knives can be used but it needs extra care.

2- Renew cloths frequently, and wash out sponges regularly.

Some upper cleaning machines are fitted with both dry and wet brushes. The machine may be fitted

a) Dry brush for welt cleaning

b) Wet brush

c) Dry brushes for cleaning off.

CLEANING DRY BY MACHINE-

The machine has an applicator for cleaner, and usually a mild water-based type is chosen for general cleaning.

1- Adjust the amount of cleaner applied to the revolving brush (drip feed) to “wet out” the material without being excessive.

2- Take care not to over brush and damage the finish.

3- Follow the following work method.

----- **Clean the feather area with the small welt cleaning brush.**

----- **Clean the upper with bigger wet brush.**

----- **Dry the upper on the cloth mop.**

----- **Polish on the woolen brush.**

4- Clean by hand any stubborn areas to avoid damage.

"WETTING OUT" AND DRYING OUT-

A cleaner to be effective must "wet out" the material being cleaned. If the liquid does not spread out on the surface, but runs over in drops, it is not wetting the finish and should not be used.

After cleaning, uppers must be allowed to thoroughly dry out before other operations are carried out. Otherwise, there will be lack of adhesion with the next coat of dressing.

CLEANING OF VARIOUS SOILING MATERIALS-

SOILING MATERIAL	CLEANING AGENT
Color code paint (on material edge)	Detergent
Thread lubricant	Detergent
Spray marking	Detergent
Elastic	Solvent
Silver pen	Solvent
Grease	Solvent/ Detergent
Styrene	Solvent
Thermoplastic- Adhesive	Blunt Knife
Rubber Adhesive	Crepe Rubber
PU Adhesive	Crepe Rubber/ Solvent
Neoprene Adhesive	Crepe Rubber

On suede leather, use only a abrasive / blunt knife or wire brush.
Apply detergent with a sponge- solvent with a rag (cloth) , rub until dry .
Always clean in circular motion.

A SELECTION OF CLEANING SOLVENTS IN GENERAL USE-

Solvent	Other names	Dissolves	Remarks
Benzene	**Benzoyl**	**Rubber, oils, fats, resins and waxes**	**Very flammable, toxic fumes**
Petroleum Naphtha **a) Petroleum ether** **b) Ligroin** **White spirit**	**Benzine, petrol, gasoline** **Light benzene, light petroleum** **Middle benzene, cleaning benzene** **Heavy benzene**	**Rubber oil, fats, resin & waxes**	**Too flammable and volatile for general use.** **Very flammable, but less volatile** **Flammable, less volatile, dilute in**

			water
Methylated spirit	Ethyl alcohol	Resins, spirit, dyes ,sewing waxes	Flammable mixes with water.
Acetone		Resins, fats, some waxes	Very flammable, partly mixes with water.
Methyl ethyl ketone	M. E. K.	Resins, fats, some waxes	Flammable, less volatile than acetone
Amyl acetate	Banana oil	Resins, fats, some waxes	Flammable, less volatile than acetone.

W RINKLE CHASING

This operation is to remove small creases that may appear after cleaning. This technique is to apply heat to the surface of the upper or lining material, to shrink the surface slightly and tightening the grain (if leather) and thereby **removing the creases.**

IRONING-

Special electrically heated hand irons, which are **thermostatically controlled are used for removing wrinkles.**

Sometimes the whole leather surface is ironed to improve finish. (**Danger**- fats etc. may surface up, the dressing coat may not adhere. Consult the supplier of shoe finishing chemicals).

PRECAUTIONS-

1- **Avoid a heat build up** in a small localized area, which may damage the finish of leather, or shrink the upper. Have **Teflon cloth** on the iron to prevent burning. Maximum temperature of the iron 70- 75 degree c and with the **Teflon cloth up to 96 degree c.** You may apply water before ironing to prevent burning or anticrease wax if water cannot be used.

2- **Patent and high gloss finishes** are very easily blistered or lose gloss in the heat. It is sometimes an advantage to apply a little Vaseline or anticreasing wax as a lubricant especially when ironing.

3- **Discoloration of pastel shades, white and aniline finishes**- All have the tendency to discolor under heat. Check the effect on scrap before attempting the bulk.

4- **High grease content leather,** the heat may bring the grease to the surface and prevent adhesion of later dressings or cause bloom to appear after boxing.

5- **Synthetics,** wrinkle chasing is relatively ineffective, and most of these materials have poor resistance to the heat.

HOT AIR BLOWER (HOT BLAST)

Hot air under pressure is directed over the surface of the material.

The machine is stationary (mounted on a bench) and the shoe is moved under the air stream.

Some of these machines have the facility to inject water spray or steam into the air jet, which is said to be beneficial to leathers by reducing the tendency to burn and promoting shrinkage.

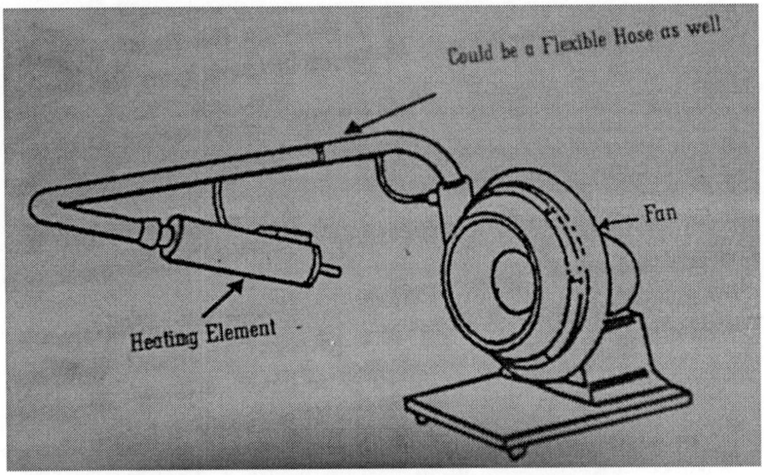

BOOT LEG TREEING MACHINE-

For good appearance, boot legs are shaped by a special treeing machine designed for the purpose.

a) Leg of the shoe is mulled by steam to make it ready for shaping.
b) Heated aluminium "legs" is inserted into the boot leg.
c) The aluminium leg is then stretched (split in the centre) to heat and give shape to the leg of the upper.
d) The leg of upper, while stretched, is also heated by radiation from the heating elements situated outside the boot for heat setting.

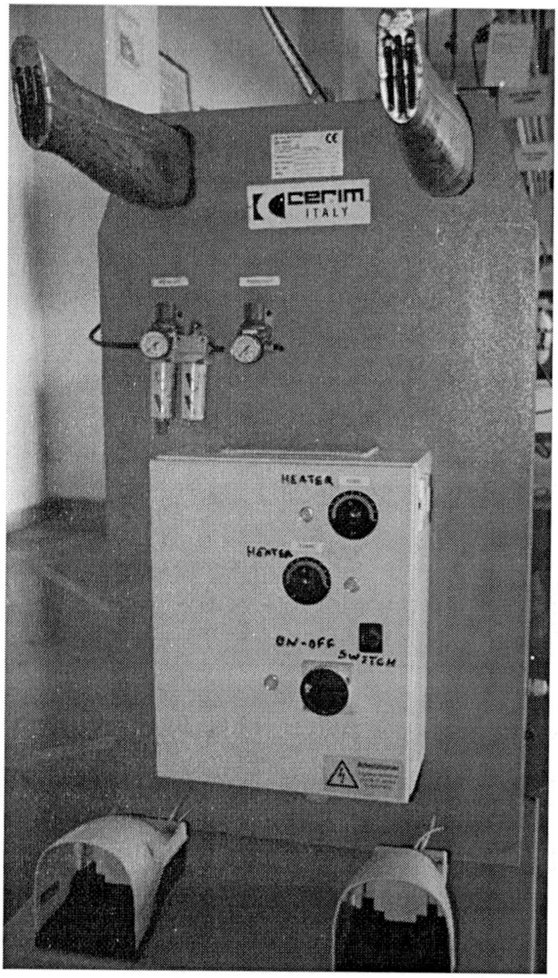

REPAIRING & UNIFORMING-

Various damages and defects on the shoes like pleating or bleeding of finish scratches, scuff damage, adhesive and solvent stains are to be rectified. Repairing or renovation is a highly skilled job. Depending upon the type and intensity of defect proper formulation is applied. Pastes are applied to damaged portions, by a brush on scratches. The material sinks into damaged portions. Pigment finishes, pastes or dyes are applied carefully. Liquid dyes are touched, to compensate color loss. Crayon is rubbed over the scratches and smoothened by a clean cloth.

During the shoe making process upper material is subjected to a variety of abrasive and stretching actions, which can adversely affect the appearance of the shoe.

The damage may be due to the following reasons-

1- Over roughing along the featheredge.
2- Scuffing of the finish during handling.
3- Damage to the finish by solvents and heat.
4- Grain crack during lasting.
5- Increase in shade variation of upper leather.

The purpose of repairing is to bring the shoe to an acceptable standard before continuing with other operations in the shoe room. It can be done by **repair crayons, repair paste and spray paints for grainy upper materials.** The paste or spray can be either water or spirit based.

Repairing includes both upper and bottom repairs, of a minor nature, such as scratched uppers at upper roughing, heat scouring and very slight cuts during upper clicking, lasting etc.

For the bottoms, main repair area may be in the heel, especially at the seat and heel breast.

The purpose of these repairs is to bring the shoe to a good standard, before continuing with the other operations in the finishing shoe room.

PRECAUTIONS-

1- Never repair deep scratches, cuts etc. on the upper as their repair will only leave marks which would be seen on the finishing shoe and therefore should not be attempted.
2- For minor scratches, cuts use very fine grit size abrasive to first even the surface, then apply repair crayons or pigment pasters and finish off with renovators etc.
3- Pigments and dyes must match the color of the upper.

4- If only the finish is damaged, use uniformers or renovators.

5- For repair of the sole use-

----- PU paint for PU soles.

----- TPR paint for TPR soles.

----- Creams and polishes + color for leather soles.

Table given below shows the main features of repairs for leather uppers-

DESCRIPTION	FORM	TYPE	METHOD OF APPLICATION	SPECIAL FEATURES

Repair crayons	Sticks, Discs	Wax based in very soft, medium & hard forms, colored	Soft crayons can be rubbed on. Hard crayons melted on with warm knife	Gap filling- will not shrink, used for heavy damage. Not suitable for flexible areas. Dry instantly on cooling.
Repair pastes	Thick paste	Colored resin emulsions.	Brush or knife	Resin sprays may not stick to repaired areas Can be matched
Unifor mers, Renovat ors	Solution or emulsion	Pigmented, solvent or waterborne	Spray or brush	Not gap filling for light damage. Dry in 5- 20 minutes. Not suitable for flexible areas.
Pigment paints	Paste	Water based	Hand brush	For slight damage on shoe feather line

Waxes & creams generally contain higher level of pigments or dyes with binder and can help the damaged surface of leather to regain a measure of its original appearance. If only the finish of the leather has been removed then good repairs are possible, but where the damage is deep into the grain the wax may not be enough to camouflage the more fibrous nature of the surface.

In the same manner for textile having polymer coatings on it. Color matching of the damaged area to the original surface, will be the only beneficial solution.

A range of fabric & leather dyes is available for "touching- up" the localized color losses or more commonly re-coloring the whole upper. With fabrics & absorbent leather such as suede & nubucks there is little preparation required but where the leather has a finish this normally has to be removed with solvents before the dye can take.

Renovators are used to blend color with rest of the shoe or even to add a color contrast according to the fashion required.

FILLING BY BASE COAT APPLICATION-

FILLERS- Fillers are base coats used to cover microporus cracks. Synthetic resin (acrylic resins) like methacrylic esters are commonly used as Fillers (in either solvent solution or water emulsion of fine particle size). Penetrating and wetting agents help the penetration of resin into the leather.

During fabrication the shoe material is subjected to various mechanical damages. Microcracks are developed normally during lasting operations. Fillers are base coats. Filler selection depends upon the finish on the material. Shoes of resin and protein finished leathers require filling.

Fillers are available either in cream or liquid form. These products are used to fill upper leathers, which have developed an **"open & hungry"** look after lasting. They act as a base coat for subsequent top dressing. They seal the surface, so that the top coat does not sink in and only minimum quantity has to be applied to give the desired appearance and beauty. Fillers also enhance the gloss and are necessary for inferior quality leather.

They are available as follows-

1- LIGHT FILLERS- (For light leather finish)

All the leathers where we use protein binders like aniline finish and semi- aniline finished leather.

2- **MEDIUM FILLERS-** (For Resin finished leather)

All the leathers which are corrected grain nature and having the resin binder and fully pigmented.

3- **HEAVY FILLERS-** For leather with open or hungry looks like garments, nappa and hand gloving manufacturing leather.

Fillers are generally used before dressing operation. It improve the appearance of the finish of some leather. It should apply by natural sponge, and sometimes by spray machine.

Some **Cream, polishes and waxes** also work as a filler in some operation and produce semi- gloss appearance to the material. They improve the feel and texture of the material. The working procedures are as follows-

1- Apply the sponge or cloth, and allow it to dry.

2- Brush on a power driven revolving cotton sheet mop.

3- Hard wax can be apply at this stage by power driven cotton sheet mop and finally polished on a power driven woolen mop 500-600 rpm.

4- Spraying is not necessary.

All the fillers are usually available in black for black leathers and colorless for other leather colors. Occasionally the base coats can be color matched which helps to lessen shade variations. They are usually applied by hand using sponges and they should dry out "steak free".

Use of correct filler will also help in cases where there are problems of adequate adhesion between the top coat and the shoe upper.

Given below are the rules for Fillers and different types of leather but these are only guides, not hard and fast rules and can be varied within limits.

Leather Finish	LEATHER	BASE OR FILLER

Protein Resin Polyurethane (PU) Polyvinyl chloride Wax Suede, Nubuck	Aniline calf, Glazed kid leather Resin Semi- aniline, Rub off, Pearlized Patent, coated split, finished split. Patent, Coated split Burnish, Oil pull- up Suede, Nubuck	Light filler where needed Any type when necessary None Only color matching can be done where finish is off. None Only color matching can be done where finish is off. Light filler if required None

BASE COAT POLISH- Apply base coat on clean shoes-

1- Remove oil, grease and other contaminations prior to application.
2- Remove dust with tack rags just prior to base coat.
3- Observe the recoat time.

After the color has been smoothly layered on the base , the next step is to polish the base coat before a clear coat. The polishing is done by using special brush. It is not a complicated process. Each time base coat done carefully. The base coat must be allowed to dry and then be re- examined for further imperfection that may have to be polished out.

A finishing may be applied by brush or spray gun, allowed to dry and then wax polished on a revolving lines mop and soft hair brushes. Alternatively, a friction wax must be used which color the sole and impregnates the surface. This also requires wax polishing. Black sole bottom requires an additional operation of brushing with a leather pad before polishing.

DRESSING-

This operation is often the final treatment which gives the shoe its luster (extra look) and determines its final appearance. Shoe dressers are top sprays, classified as water based, solvent based and cellulose based. The formulations contain in addition to natural or synthetic resin, soap, essential oils and a plasticizer. Cellulose dressing is prepared by dissolving shellac in a suitable solvent like butanol and mixed with cellulose ester. Shoe finish is applied on the surface of the shoe by a brush or spray. The type of dressing formulation sprayed depends upon the type of leather and the fashion trend.

The success of dressing depends upon-

1- Correct and thorough cleaning.
2- Compatibility of the dressing with the material finish.
3- Condition of the upper before applying the dressing.
4- Correct application.
5- Correct spray gun adjustment and technique.

TYPES OF DRESSINGS AND APPLICATIONS-

Water based dressing-

Water based dressings are mainly wax emulsions, or blends of wax with resin, polyurethane or acrylics. They are colorless as well as with colors. The modern sprays are made from acrylic resin emulsions and are suitable for use on protein and nitrocellulose coated leathers but not for polyurethane. **Liquid dressing** are of two types: wax based and PU based.

Wax based dressing requires brushing, which gives a natural shine to the shoe.

PU based dressing normally does not require brushing. It gives an artificial shine.

Both wax- based and PU based dressing can be applied by hand or by spray.

1- Check compatibility of the dressing with the upper material because non compatibility shows as **cracks, peel off or white marks.**
2- Apply dressing by hand or spraying according to finishing system selected.

Solvent based dressings-

Solvent- based dressings from strong coating, which are compatible with a wide range of upper materials. They are fast drying and are based on cellulose derivatives, acrylics or polyurethane. They can be clear or colored and are available in a wide range of luster (extra look) from matt to high gloss. Normally waxes dyes etc. are mixed with or dissolved in solvents. These form liquids or semi liquids (pastes). Solvents enable them to be spread and may assist with penetration. They must be applied with spray and give very bright colorfast finish.

1- Check compatibility of the dressing with the upper material because non- compatibility shows as **crack, peel off or white marks.**
2- Apply dressing by hand or spraying according to finishing system selected.

CREAMS, POLISHERS AND WAXES-

Such products are non- film forming. Normally wax polishes are used and are widely available either neutral or pigmented to match the color. Surface waxes can impart a measure of water repellency to footwear although they can not be regarded as water proofing agents. They will help against light showers but persistent water contact will soon penetrate the wax particularly where flexing breaks the surface layers.

Waxes and creams are also suitable for gloss enhancement or to give some special appearance (antique effect) on leather look synthetic material. **Creams could be soft, medium or hard.** Soft and medium creams are those that require to be polished and are referred to as the **creams to be polished. Hard creams are available as self- finishing creams. They do not require cutting or brushing operation.**

These can only impart some semi- gloss appearance to the material. However, they improve the feel and handle of the materials.

Silicones have been introduced in the creams for patents to prevent the shoes from sticking to each other as can happen in the shoe box.

Process=

1- Apply by sponge or cloth, allow it to dry.
2- Brush on a power driven revolving cotton sheet mop.

Hard waxes (upper wax) can be applied at this stage by power driven cotton sheet mop and finally polished on a power driven woolen mop, 500 – 600 rpm.

Spray is not necessary.

CLEANERS / POLISHES-

Cleaner/ polishes are supplied as gels or creams, and contain solvent cleaners and polishing agents. Which remain on the surface after the solvents have evaporated. These are very suitable for patents and PU coated fabrics, and have the advantage of giving an acceptable semi- bright finish without having to spray.

Apply by sponge or cloth.

After drying it can be polished on a power driven woolen mop, 500 – 600 rpm.

WAXES-

Waxes are valuable ingredient for shoe finishes, dressings, polish, pastes, creams and repairers. Carnauba wax of vegetable origin, paraffin wax obtained from mineral oil and bees wax of insect origin are widely used. In practice a homogeneous mixture of two or more waxes are used in polishes/ finishes. They can be colored (pigmented). Wax pastes are prepared when a mixture of waxes are dissolved in Turpentine or any other suitable solvents. Shoe creams are prepared from waxes by emulsifying them with turpentine and water rendered alkaline by soap or synthetic emulsifiers. Essential oil are used as additives. Wax crayons used as repairers are white or colored waxes blocked into sticks of size 10 x 1 cm. Waxes are usually used for Burnishing, Repairing & polishing. They are of different types and having different properties-

ABRASIVE WAX-

Abrasive wax is used for cutting or smoothening of grain surface, and for filling and provide the special effect on the surface of the shoe.

This operation is required for finishing of leather and to give shinning or polishing effect on upper leather. This is also converting the course grain leather into fine grain leather. To provide or bring the burnishing effect or brush- off effect.

CHARACTERISTICS-

1- High smooth finish and provide good and durable gloss.
2- It provides the better cutting effect.
3- It is found both solid and liquid form. Liquid abrasive penetrates in the leather fibers and enhance its natural color and give wet look.

REPAIRING WAX-

Actually repairing wax are gap- filling crayons and do not shrink on flexing. Repairing waxes are two types-

1- Soft wax
2- Hard wax

1- SOFT WAX- For rapid repair of scratches and minor defects on many surfaces in the area of least wear and tear.

2- HARD WAX- For a more permanent hard wearing repair to busy areas and delicate surfaces such as foils and prints with a heat resistance up to 110 degree c, this wax is suitable.

POLISHING WAX-

Polishing wax used as the final operations to polish and protect the finish that is done in the shoe finishing room. It also enhance the gloss of the shoe. It is also two types-

1- Carnauba wax
2- Synthetic wax

This type of wax is required for finishing of leather shoes to provide shining or polishing effect on upper leather. This is also converting or merges the course grain leather into fine grain upper leather. To provide or bring the burnishing effect, two tone effect, polishing effect to the upper leather.

Sometimes abrasive wax is a good polishing wax to provide the high gloss on the surface of the shoes. It is found in different color and used as the color of the article to provide a thin layer with the help of brushing machine.

BRUSHING MACHINE- Generally this operation carried out in shoe room with the help of burnishing machine, with provision for cotton and woolen brushing, for cutting and polishing purpose.

In polishing, normally use roller of brushing machine at low speed with the use of polishing with synthetic wax or carnauba wax.

Where as when high abrasive action is not required then rollers of brushing machine at medium speed with the use of abrasive wax.

CHARACTERISTICS-

1- It provides high smooth finish with good durable gloss.
2- It provides the good cutting effect.
3- It is found both in solid and liquid form.

For liquid abrasive, it penetrates in the pores of the leather and enhance its natural color and give wet look.

BURNISHING WAX-

It is a medium – hard dyed wax, which enhance the burnishing effect on burnished leather.

PROTECTORS-

These are liquids, which is normally applied by aerosol spray, confer on the footwear material a measure of water/ oil repellency and hence reduce the severity of subsequent staining. The depth of absorption and hence the degree of protection depends upon the absorbency of the material. They are therefore most popular for unfinished leathers like suedes and nubucks. The most common repellency agents used in these formulations are silicon oils and fluorocarbons, which are both highly hydrophobic. Again however, their efficiency is short lived and hence need regular reapplications. They may also cause significant darkening on lighter colored materials and may not protect light colored uppers from heavy or dark stains. These treatments are also well suited to textiles particularly those containing natural fibers.

BRUSH OFF FINISH-

For brush off effect, the leather is having two coats of color of different shades. The top most coat is partly brushed off in shoe finishing.

1- Apply a hard abrasive wax (cutting wax) on to a power driven revolving cotton sheet mop, partly brush off the top most color coating to bring about the brush off look.
2- Further brushing, when necessary, can be done by applying a **filler wax** onto the revolving cotton sheet mop, and brush the surface of the leather.
3- Finally, polish on power driven woolen mop.

ANTIQUE FINISH-

Antique effects can enhance the appearance of the shoe.

1- Apply an antique cream by sponge or cloth.

Or

1- Spray the antique cream (emulsified).
2- Immediately wipe off the cream. Some of the darker shade cream is left on seam and bunched edges and stitches to achieve the effect.

SHADOW FINISH-

Shadow finish is fairly similar to the antique finish.

1- Spray somewhat darker color along the leather edge, perforations etc. to bring about the shadow effect.

TREATMENTS COMBINED (LEATHER UPPERS)

Leather finish	Cleaning	Filling	Repairing	Dressing
RESIN	Solvent or water based	Water & solvent	Use wax crayons or	Solvent and water based

	cleaners. May be hand or machine cleaned.	based cleaners are available. Not always necessary.	pigments for scratches and scuffs. If only finish is damage use uniformers.	dressing are suitable. If finish is filled, water based dressings are best.
ANILINE	Miled water based cleaners or mild nonionic detergent cleaners.	Not usually necessary but special fillers are available if required.	Can be very difficult special aniline repair sticks are available.	Water based dressing are preferred, keep dressing quantity to a minimum. Wax emulsion polishes may be applied by hand or brush.
PATENT OR PVC	Solvent based are best. Special cleaner polishes are available.	Not necessary	Solvent based repairs are available.	No top dressing is necessary. Cream or special cleaner are available.
PROTEIN	Water and solvent	Water based are	As for resin	Water based dressing is

	based cleaner are suitable.	preferred.		preferred.
EASY-CARE	Solvent based	Not necessary	Solvent based preferred but may be difficult.	Solvent based, creams but little dressing should be required.
RUBB- OFF	Mild water based cleaners.	Not necessary	As for resin using a color similar to original rub-off.	Solvent base dressing are preferred.
SUEDE AND NUBUCK	Brushing	Not necessary	Suede color powder to match the shade.	Colored & water proffing sprays.

THE TREATMENT OF SYNTHETIC (man- made) UPPERS-

SYNTHETIC MATERIAL	CLEANING	REPAIRING	DRESSING
Polyvinyl chloride (PVC) coated fabric	Solvent based preferred. Special cleaner/ polishes are available. Hand cleaning	Some hard repair sticks are available. Solvent based repairs should be	Solvent-based dressings are available but are not usually necessary. Creams/cleaner polishes for

	recommended.	used. Repairing is difficult.	general cleaning and finishing are available.
POLYURETHANE COATED FABRICS (P.U.C.F.)	As for PVC	Not usually possible	As for PVC
POROMERICS	As above	Solvent-based renovators and repairers should be used. Repairing is difficult.	Solvent based dressing are generally used but some water based dressings are available. Creams/ cleaner polishes are usually adequate.

PROBLEMS ENCOUNTERED IN THE UPPER FINISHING-

PROBLEM	POSSIBLE CAUSES	PREVENTION OR CURE
1- Flaking of shoe finishing dressing. (This is when the dressing starts to peel off).	Material finish and dressing incompatible. Excessive stearate in finish. Dressing fails to wet out the leather finish.	Check suitability of dressing before use. Try stronger cleaner to prepare the leather finish.

	Excessive build up of cleaner solids in dirty sponges or clothes. Inadequate cleaning particularly after use of cutting or polishing wax. Contamination from other operations. .	Keep cleaners free from contamination and wash or disregard sponges or clothes regularly. Clean more thoroughly. Possibly change to stronger cleaner. Identify and eliminate sources of contaminations.
2- Crazing of shoe finish dressing. (This is when the dressing cracks)	Dressing coat too thick. Dressing coat too brittle. Dressing de- plastics on ageing.	Spray correct thickness. Change to less brittle coating. Check storage of shoe. Very warm or cold storage not recommended.
3- BLOOM -----Salt ------ Fat	Leather too salty. Excessive fat content	Clean with damp cloth.

(This is a dullness which may appear as a grayish streak on the surface of the leather).	in leather.	Reduce fat content. Change to alternative finishing system.
	Heat causes fat to move to leather surface.	Avoid excessive heat in shoe making. Warm gently to disperse bloom.
	Solvent from cleaner or dressing causes fat to move to the surface of leather.	Hot air treatment or spraying with high boiling point solvents.
	High atmospheric humidity	Dry brushing is quite effective in removing bloom.
-------moisture (spue)	Inadequate cleaning off of cutting or polishing wax.	Clean more thoroughly, possibly change to stronger cleaner.
----solvent induced	High atmospheric humidity.	Dry brushing can some times be effective.
	Water in solvents. Water in upper	Modify the solvent blend with excessive moisture.
	Movement of soluble to surface of upper	

	Partial softening of leather finish leading to incorrect film properties or drying.	Spray affected areas with high boiling point solvent. Change to alternative finishing system.
4- Dried dressing film is uneven.	Poor wetting of material finish. Dressing contaminated with water or oil. Filler coats, if used, too dry. Faulty spraying, e.g. pressure, fluid flow, pattern. Atmospheric contaminations from other factory areas. Too much dressing applied.	Use more effective cleaner. Attend to drainage and air controller pressure on air line. Reduce drying time of filter- never overnight. Keep guns and gauges in working order. Needles are prone to damage. Check contamination from other factory areas.
5- Tackiness of dried dressing.	Incorrect dressing used with upper finish.	Check compatibility first.

	Over spray onto other components may turn tacky.	Mask or clean off after spraying.
6- Tissue paper sticking to PVC upper or sole edge.	Boxing before dressing has not dried sufficiently. Use of dressing which is softened by PVC plasticisers. Abnormality in PVC uppers Abnormality in PVC soling	Increase time between spraying and drying. Change to dressing formulated to be resistant to PVC plasticisers. Change to another PVC Change to another PVC or mask the soling or clean off dressing from sole edge before boxing.

MATERIALS, TOOLS AND EQUIPMENTS USED IN SHOE FINISHING OPERATIONS-

1- SOAP OR DETERGENT-

Detergent and soaps are used for cleaning because pure water can not remove oily and organic soiling. Soaps cleans by acting as an emulsifier. Basically soaps allows oil and water to mix so that oily grims can be removed during rinsing.

Detergents are primarily surfactants, which could be produced easily from petrochemicals. Surfactants, lower the surface tension of water, easily wet back and quickly remove the oil and greases.

Modern detergent contains more than surfactants. Cleaning products may also contains enzymes to degrade protein based stains, bleaches to de color stains and add power to cleaning agents. Detergents are similar to soap, but they are less form films and are not yet effected by the presence of materials in the hard water.

2-SOLVENT CLEANERS-

The solvent in this type are usually derived from petroleum and can be mixed with other solvents of the same type to give different cleaning power. These are suitable for removing grease, oils and waxes. They are very quick in drying. Solvents cleaners are petrol, disel and kerosene oil. Kerosene oil is mixed with solvent emulsion type cleaners for softening heavy preservatives coating. It is also used to general solvent cleaning, but its use should be followed by a coating or rinse with some other type of protective agent. Kerosene does not evaporate as rapidly as dry cleaning solvents. Kerosene film may be removed with safety solvents, water emulsions, cleaners or detergents mixture.

3-POLISHERS-

Polishers are supplied as gels and contains solvent cleaners and polishing agents, which remains on the surface after the solvents have evaporated.

Application is by sponge or cloth and after drying can be polished on a power mob machine. These are very suitable for patent and PU coated fabrics, and have the advantage of giving an acceptable semi- bright finish without having to spray.

4-CONDITIONERS-

Conditioners are water based and designed to open up the surface for efficient cleaning. Cleaning can be done both wet and dry method either by hand or by machine.

CLEANING BY HAND-

The items used for this cleaning methods are-

1- **CREPE RUBBER- For** removing adhesive.
2- **SOFT SPONGE RUBBER-** Brushing the suede nap.
3- **BRUSHES-** Wire and stiff bristle type.
   --- For removing general dust and dirt from suede.
   --- For brushing up the suede nap.

5-POLISHING WAX-

Melting point 78 – 81 degree c.

Polishing wax used as the final operations to polish and protect the finish that is done in the shoe finishing room. It also enhance the gloss and beauty of the shoes. It is also two types-

1- Carnauba wax
2- Synthetic wax

6-TOP COAT POLISH-

Top coat provides the gloss, appearance and protect the leather from damage. It also give the feel and aesthetic appeal.

The final coat is usually free from resin is design to increase fastness to wet and dry rubbing and help to obtain adequate resistance to hot platting. Small quantities of wax preparation are also used to obtain a warm feel to the best possible surface smoothness. Gloss can be controlled in a suitable manner by the thickness of the finish film. The finishing coat are hardened with dilute formaldehyde or mixture of formaldehyde to get the water proof leather.

PROPERTIES-1

1-The top coat protect the shoe from damage due to rubbing and scratches.

2-To provide level appearance of color.

3-To provide suitable shade and burnishing and two tone effects as per the fashion and market requirements.

4-To retains its properties during the all shoe manufacturing operations and could be easily dressed.

5-To be easily cleaned and polished.

6-Durability against rubbing on dry and wet.

7-Permeability to water vapor and air, ensuring that hygienic properties.

8-Should be fast to stain and light.

9-Should not crack on being extended or flexed.

10-Resistance to heat, cold and moisture.

11-Durability of the finish in wear.

12-To protect the layer against adverse chemicals.

7-REPAIRING WAX-

Repairing wax are gap filling crayons and do not shrink on flexing. These are-

1- Repair crayons

2- Repair paste
3- Uniformers, Renovators
4- Pigment paints.

The purpose of repairing is to bring the shoe to an acceptable standard before continuing with other operations in the shoe room. It can be done by repair crayons, repair pastes and spray points for grainy upper materials. The paste or spray can be either water or spirit base.

Repairing includes both upper and bottom repairs, of a minor nature. The purpose of these repairing waxes is to bring the shoe to a good standard, before continuing with the other operations in the finishing.

Waxes and creams generally contain higher level of pigments or dyes with binder and can help the damage surface of the leather to regain a measure of its original appearance. If only the finish of the leather has been removed good repairs are possible, but where the damage is deep into the grain the wax may not be enough fulfil the more fibrous nature of the surface.

REPAIR CRAYONS-

It is available in sticks or Discs form. It is soft crayons, based in very soft, medium and hard form of color. It is used for gap filling of heavy damage. It is not suitable for flexible area.

REPAIRING PASTE-

It is available in thick paste form. It is colored resin emulsion used on brush or knife. It is not filling the gap properly for light damage. Dry to 15 – 20 minutes and not suitable for flexible area.

UNIFORMERS, RENOVATORS-

It is available in solution or emulsion form. It is pigmented, solvent or waterborne form and applied with spray/ brush.

PIGMENT PAINTS-

It is in paste form and water based, applied with hand brushes. It is suitable for light damage on shoe feather line.

Repairing waxes are two types-

1- **Soft waxes**
2- **Hard waxes**

SOFT WAXES- For rapid repair of scratches and minor defects on many surface in area of least wear and tear.

HARD WAXES- For a more permanent hard wearing repair to busy areas and delicate surfaces, such as foils and prints with a heat resistance up to 110 degree c, this wax is suitable.

8-SOLE EDGE COLOR-

A water base edge containing pigment waxes and gums is applied by hand to the sole edge. A machine may also be used. The edge must be completed and evenly covered with the ink, but there must be no ink on the upper and stitching.

Sole edge colors are very important to improve the appearance of the bottom parts of the shoe, with application of these coloring materials, the water resistance of the heel increases. Its final appearance is like shined looks a original finish on heels and soles.

FEATURES AND DIRECTIONS-

1- Shake well before use with cap on.
2- Shoe must be clean and dry.
3- Invert bottle and gently press applicator against shoe to release product.
4- Spread polish evenly and allow to dry to a shine.
5- Rinse applicator with water after use and blot dry to keep foams soft, replace cap.
6- If spilled, clean up before dry, gently remove spill with a dry cloth.

9-BASE COAT POLISH-

After the color has been smoothly layered on the base, the next step is to polish a base coat before a clear coat. The polishing is done by using special brush. It is not a complicated process. Each time base coat done carefully, the base coat must be allowed to dry and then be reexamined for further imperfection that may have to be polished out.

Apply base coat on clean primer.

----- Remove oil, grease and other contamination prior to application.

----- Remove dust with tack rags just prior to base coat.

---- Observe the recoat time.

A finish may be applied by brush or spray gun, allowed to dry and then wax polished on a revolving linen mop and soft hair brushes. Alternatively, a friction wax may be used which colors the sole and impregnates the surface. This also requires wax polishing. Black sole bottoms require an additional operation of brushing with a leather pad before polishing.

BOTTOM OR SOLE FINISHES-

The edges and bottom of the soles and heels are rendered attractive by bottom finishes. Gum stains are gums or a mixture of gums and waxes dissolved in alcohol, sole dressings are water based resins and waxes. Heel finishing chemicals consists of water based finish followed by a solvent based resin finish and a heel stain- an edge finish consisting of waxes and gums. Edge inks are water based compositions containing wax gums, pigment to color or acrylic emulsions containing aniline dyes.

LEATHER SOLES AND HEEL FINISHING-

a) **Heel Pairing-** Excess of material around the heel is removed, and the heel is correctly shaped, using elliptical cutters running at a speed of 6000 to 7000 r.p.m.
b) **Heel scour-** Scratches and knife marks on the heel surface are removed by means of rollers fitted with abrasive paper.
c) **Edge pairing-** The excess of material from the edge of the sole is removed using high speed rotary cutters.
d) **Bottom skiving-** Sole are snuffed on grain side using Naumkeag, a rotating disc of rubber pad covered with a fine grade abrasive.

In all these operations, the soles and heels are shaped to the correct dimensions. Ensure left and right components are of same shape, with smooth surfaces and without damaging the upper. They are dusted before the finish is applied.

EDGE SET- Wax is applied around the edge of the sole. They are positioned on to the heated oscillating irons. The wax melts and is forced into the fibrous structure of the soles giving a shiny appearance and at the same time renders the edge waterproof.

EDGE INKING- The edge of soles are uniformly colored using edge inks. These formulations are made from waxes, gums and pigment.

SOLE FINISHING- A gum stain is applied by sponge and dried. Wax from a block is applied to a revolving linen mop. The soles are at first exposed on to this mop and then on to revolving soft hair brush.

HEEL FINISH- The heels are given a coat of aqueous based finish, followed by a coat of solvent based finish, with in between drying. Both the finishes are applied by means of suitable brushes. The heels are smoothened by exposing them against revolving superfine abrasive. Heels are then gummed. Subsequently the heel is polished over a revolving brush to which a suitable wax is applied from a block.

NUBUCK AND SUEDE CARE AND SPRAYS-

Some leather are buffed and brushed to produce a soft surface with a fuzzy texture. Suede is split leather that has been buffed on its inner side, the side of the hide that was closest to the flesh of the animal. Nubuck is top grain leather that has been buffed on its outer side, the side of the hide on which the animals hair grew. Nubuck can also be made from full grain leather. Because nubuck is made from the strong outer layer of the hide, it is more durable than suede.

Suede is made from animal skin by buffing its inner surface with emery to turn out a soft, napped finish that can also be dyed. Suede is a thinner and more flexible material than leather and can not withstand precipitation and typical leather cleaning. A few drop of water can change suede, softness into an uneven, discolored, stiff and stained fabric, so that it requires a different type of cleaning.

Suede leather can be cleaned with a vinegar- water solution or polished with standard shoe shining liquid. Before wearing suede, spray on a light application of silicon, if it has not been previously treated. This will help to repel water. When dry restore suede nap very gently rubbing with fine sand paper. Do not rub too hard or too much, or you will remove the nap completely.

PROTECT YOUR NUBUCK/ SUEDE-

1- Spray the entire surface of the dry leather lightly and evenly with a water and stain repellent specially made for suede and nubuck.
2- Apply a second coat after the first one has dried.
3- Re- apply protect and after any exposure to water. Allow the leather to dry thoroughly before application.
4- Remove any dry surface dirt with a nubuck cloth or brush by rubbing the leather gently.
5- Rub a nubuck stain eraser softly against any stains.
6- Brush the nubuck first, spray the leather with the cleaner, and then rub it with a nubuck cloth.
7- Apply a special leather degreaser for oily stains such as greases, butter or body oil.
8- Apply special conditioners made for napped or oiled nubuck.

SPRAYS FOR SUEDE AND NUBUCK-

There are three main spray treatment for suede and nubuck-

1- The spraying of a fixative solution to fix the glazed power on the surface of the suede/ nubuck to improve the nap.
2- In the case of black color, a high staining dye may be used to ensure the absolute uniformity of color.
3- Suede pig skins may be treated with an expensive coating to improve water repellency. In this case a special spray gun has to

be used and strict safety precautions must be exercised because of the toxic nature of the liquid.

The characteristics of this leather is the velvety effect due to raised naps on the surface which gives **"Writing effect"** on the surface.

LIQUID POLISH-

Polish usually contains several kinds of waxes, paraffins waxes, resin, solvents, auxiliary agents and water. As well as the requirements of the consumer, cost of the components is an important factors in the formulations.

Liquid polish used as a protector, which is normally applied by spray to repell the water/ oil penetration and avoid the formation of stains. The depth of absorption and hence the degree of protection depends upon the absorbency of the material.

POLISHING INSTRUCTIONS-

Polishing should take no more than a few minutes-

1- Start by removing any dirt or contaminants by wiping the shoe with a damp cloth or sea sponge.
2- Apply a small amount of shoe cream and apply evently in a circular motion over shoes. You can see either cotton cloth or polish application brush to apply.
3- Take a minute to allow the shoe cream time to dry on each shoes.
4- Once dry use polishing cloth or polishing pad for high shine.

TIPS AND TRICKS-

1- Try and match the polish as close as you can to the color of your shoes.
2- If you choose the color neutral, use this on light colored shoes only as it tends to leave a white film on dark colored shoes.

3- Place shoes in shoe trees, this provides a film surface to polish on.
4- Always remove shoe laces before polishing to give the tongue of the shoe a good clean and ensure that your shoe laces do not get stained by the polish.
5- If the shoe has stains or greasy oil marks on them, use " **spot stain remover**" before polishing.

EMERY PAPER-

Emery paper is a type of paper that can be used for sanding down hard and rough surfaces. Emery also called iron spinel or hercynite. Emery paper is sold in sheets of varying sizes. Emery products choose on the base of the level of abrasiveness or grit. Vary course versions are designed for sanding large areas of rusts. They can be identified by their grit numbers, which ranges between 40 & 50. Medium 50 – 90.

Fine paper is the least course and has a grit value greater than 90.

POLISHING METHODS OF SHOE-

Get into the habit of polishing your leather shoes regularly. A polish conditions and helps retain leathers natural oils. It marks scuffs and enhances the color and provide a protective layer from light rain and spills.

POLISHING INSTRUCTIONS-

Polishing should take no more than a few minutes-

1- Start by removing any dirt or debris by wiping your shoes with a damp cloth.
2- Apply a small amount of shoe cream and spread evently in a circular motion over shoes. You can use either cotton cloth or a polish application brush to apply.
3- Take a minute to allow the shoe cream time to dry on each shoe.

4- Once dry, buff off with a polishing cloth or polishing pad for high shine.

TIPS AND TRICK-

1- Try and match the polish as close as you can to the color of your shoe.
2- If you choose the color neutral, use this on light colored shoes only as it tends to leave a white film on dark colored shoe over time.
3- Place shoes in shoe trees, this provides a firm surface to polish on.
4- Always remove shoe laces before polishing to give the tongue of the shoe a good clean and ensures that your shoe laces do not get stained by the polish.
5- If your shoe have stains or greasy oil marks on them use " **spot stain remover"** before polishing.

INKING BRUSHES

Brushes are differ greatly in terms of size, texture, material and cost. These are stalk, Hairs source. It is made from Goat, Siberian weasel, Pig, Mouse, Buffalo, Wolf and rabbit hair while exotic ones can be made from tiger, fowl, deer and even human hair (From the first hair cut a baby gets, said to bring good fortune while taking the imperial examinations). For good brushes its texture should be soft.

SIZE OF BRUSHES-

It should be available I different sizes;

1- Big
2- Medium
3- Small

The smallest brushes are used for very small pieces and for fashioning designs for seals. Medium brushes are most widely used by the skilled because it can produce a variety of thickness of line, from very thin to fairy thick. The larger brushes are used only for very large pieces.

SEA SPONGES-

Sea sponges have evolved over the last 500 million years and now include between 5,000 and 10,000 species variations. The majority of sponges live in salt water with only 150 species surviving in fresh water alone. While sea sponges are classified as animals, they have pigments of Chlorophyll, making them similar to many plants and bacteria species. There are four class of sea sponges-

1- Horn sponges
2- Tropical reef sponges
3- Gloss sponges
4- Calcerous sponges

It is difficult to pin down the exact number of sponge species as many distinctive species have been named more than once and new species continue to be found. While there are close to 10,000 different names for species of sponges, it is more likely that there are 6,000 actual different species. Sponges are found in a wide variety of shapes, from blob- like formations to cones and tubes, and vary in size from as small as a few millimeters to as much as two meter in height.

There are only about six species of sea sponges that are sold commercially as bath sponges. These species are selected for their dense make- up and flexible skelton. In their natural environment, these sponges are black, however, they are placed into acidic solutions to decalcify the skeletons and then bleached to remove the color. A lot of sponges are used in footwear industry to apply proper color and shoes auxiliaries on the surface to increase look and appearance.

SUEDE BRUSH WIRE-

Suede brush cleans and brushes up the knap in the suede. If the suede is shiny use a little piece of 120 grit sand paper which bring up the knap even more.

In this process, we use KIWI shoe brush 100% horse hair, they provide the high gloss shine in suede leather. Similarly, we use shoe shine cloth, it should use after polishing your shoes with brush, it provides extra- bright high gloss shine. The bars removes shiny marks and stains. The brush brings the knap of the leather to its original appearance.

Suede and nubuck wire brush to raise the knap of the leather on shoes, boots, handbags or any other suede/ nubuck items. Especially good for reaching hard – to- get place.

For the cleaning of suede and nubuck product we use the following products for their long life preservations-

1- Suede and nubuck cleaner
2- Suede and nubuck protector

SUEDE AND NUBUCK CLEANER- The cleaners cleans, conditions and softens suede and nubuck leather. Removes dust and dirt from shoes, boots. Belts, clothing and more. The cleaners built- in bristle top makes application and cleaning easy and mess free.

SUEDE AND NUBUCK PROTECTOR- It provides protection sgainst water and stains. Keep suede and nubuck shoes, boots, coats, bags etc. looking new. Coats, footwear with a special polymer that creates an invisible shield to provide maximum protection against water and stains.

BLUNT KNIFE-

In the lasting operation, the complete surface of the bottom of the shoe is coated with a rubber solution or thermoplastic adhesive (Hot melt). The blunt knife is used to remove wax and thermoplastic adhesive (Hot melt). Could be used on suede and nubuck leather as a repair work.

CREPE AND RESIN RUBBER-

Generally used to remove polyurethanes, latex and rubber adhesives from grained upper and lining.

ADVANTAGES-

1- It is comparatively cheap.
2- It has good wear resistance.
3- It has self- sealing ability and provides a very good resistance to flex crack but slip on dry surface.
4- It is very light in weight.

DISADVANTAGES-

1- It is very sensitive to heat becomes soft and sticky in warm condition.
2- It has poor resistance to ageing. In the action of sun light its surface becomes hard.
3- It is sensitive to solvents mainly petroleum and oil.

INKING BRUSHES-

In footwear, the brushes are used to color the edges. A water based edge finish containing pigment, waxes and gums is applied by hand to the sole edge. The edge must be completely and evenly covered with ink, but there must be no ink on the upper and sole. The flesh side of the sole has a ¼ inch margin of ink applied. This is done to minimize the danger level, where the ink being applied to the upper when the sole in edge ink during finishing.

These brushes are differ greatly in terms of size, texture, material and cost. It is made from goat, pig, mouse, buffalo, wolf and rabbit hair while exotic once can be made from tiger, deer and even human hair. The inking brushes are three types. These are a) Big size brushes b) Medium size brushes c) Small size brushes.

LIQUID SHOE POLISH-

Liquid shoe polish usually contains several kinds of synthetic waxes, paraffin waxes, resin, solvents, auxiliary agent and water. As well as then requirement of the consumer, cost of the components is an important factors in the formulations. While shoe finishing are non- commonly and loosely referred to as inks and stains may more chemical product are in general use in shoe factories as essential raw materials for finishing purpose. In big cities polishes are used for both shining the shoes and protecting them against dust etc. In all types of color and design these are needed for polishing any kind of shoes.

Shoe polish is a waxy paste cream or liquid used to polish, shine, water proof and restore the appearance of leather shoes or boots thereby extending the footwear life.

Various substances have been used as shoe polish for hundreds of years, starting with natural substances such as wax and tallow. Modern polish formulas were introduced early in the 20th century and many of those original formulations are still in use today. Shoe polish is usually made from a mix of natural and synthetic materials including Naptha, turpentine, dyes and gum Arabic using a chemical processes. Shoe polish is usually flammable, can be toxic and if misused, can stain skin. It should be used in a well- ventilated area with care taken to protect clothes, carpets and furniture.

Shoe polish should apply on shoes with using brush. Shoe polish is not a cleaning product, therefore the footwear should be both clean and dry before application.

FINISHING FAULTS-

1-STAINS ON UPPER-

During finishing operation, like incorrect dressing, Uneven cleaning, contaminated dressing as well as atmospheric contaminations.

Due to above reasons generally faults like stains found on the upper surface of the finishing surface, because of tackiness and not proper penetration of finishes as well as en- even drying of film.

This problem also arises due to poor spray pattern, due to shaking of liquid or seasons not done before apply it on the surface.

DERERMINE THE TYPES OF LEATHER- 1- Put a drop of water on the surface of the leather, if the water soaks in the leather is un- finished and will requires more chemicals. If it breads up, the leather is finished and you can begin cleaning.

2-Take unfinished leather (like suede) directly to a dry cleaner for stain removal- unfinished leather is extremely absorbent and the stain will be very difficult to remove.

DETERMINE THE DEPTH OF THE STAIN-

1- If the stain is fresh and only on the surface of the leather item, begin cleaning according to the steps.
2- If the stain is older or has soaked into the leather, you will likely have to redye the leather professionally to remove the stain.

CLEANING-

1- Read carefully the instruction of leather, if possible because the manufacturer may recommended a certain conditioner or cleaner to remove stain.
2- Wipe the leather gently with a cloth dampened with hot spray water or use a leather shampo to clean the affected area. Treat your leather on a regular basis with quality protection products.

UNEVEN SHINE-

This fault arises due to uneven dressing, cutting, as well as un-even polishing. Apart from this using un- appropriate wax as per the finish on leather surface also results as un- even shine on the upper.

Besides this different absorptions of dye or finish on different parts of skin and hide also cause uneven shine. In correct adjustment of the spray gun applying the final coat or top coat also results as uneven shine. Then, there is possibility of low gloss and shine as well as full appearance of shoe upper. And finally we can not get the required quality in finished shoe.

One of the reasons that leather is so popular is that in addition to its great natural richness, it also take well to a large variety of finishes. There is literally something for every person taste. **Uneven shine** finish is called distressed type of finishes. In this finish a combination of physically "distressing" the leather. For example, the process might include using a hair brush and then applying wipes of pigment to produce an uneven color. The goal is to make a items look old or worn.

Another way to distress leather is to spot with water and then as it dries, it will shrink slightly giving it a pinched look. If you prefer, you can simply wear it and let natural take its course.

STREAKS ON UPPER-

In shoe room, during finishing on upper, faults like streaks on upper occurs. Normally this faults arises during liquid dressing due to uneven spray pattern. Distribution of finishing during cleaning and filling i.e. if cleaning and filling does not done properly as per quality and standard norms.

This faults also arise due to spray gun not square to work.

When leather is new, it has a rich smooth appearance, overtime the leather will begin to fade in spots where it is repeatedly worn. The color will appear uneven, with light streaks appearing through out the leather.

This often happens to leather furniture, such as on the seats or leather jackets at the crease of the arm. Fortunately, a warn leather finish can be restored to an almost new appearance with the right materials.

INSTRUCTIONS-

1- Apply a leather cleaners to a clean rag. Wipe the entire surface of the leather item to be cleaned. This is not only removes the surface dirt, but it opens the pores in the material, allowing the re-coloring balm to work more effectively.

2- Select a re- coloring balm in the appropriate shade. The shade usually come in a few basic colors and can fit a range to shades in that color family.

3- Apply the balm to a clean cloth. Beginning at the top of the item to be restored, rub the cloth in a circular pattern. This will work the color into the leather. As the color seeps into the pores, the streaks will disappear and the color will be restored. Add additional amount of balm to the cloth as necessary.

4- Buff the leather surface with a clean cloth once the entire item has been covered with the balm. Continue buffing until there is no longer a color transfer between the item and the cloth. The buffing will create a smooth, even appearance.

5- Apply a leather cream to protect your leather item against further wear and fading.

WHITENESS OCCURS IN FINISHING SHOE

In shoe finishing operation, first of all cleaning operation is done to clean the dirt, dust and other contaminants present on the surface of the shoe. Cleaners are used in cleaning operation, it should be water base, water and solvent base or totally solvent base. The type of cleaners depends upon the type of leather and quality of finishing. If water base cleaners are used then a lot of moisture content absorb on the leather fiber. If the moisture is not dry well and we apply required creams on the surface of the shoe, then due to excess moisture content in inside fiber, the gloss or final appearance of the shoe will be dull and after some times it gives white appearance on the surface of the shoe.

Sometimes, fat- liquors penetrate inside the leather fiber and after sudden variations of temperature or we export the shoe in cold countries, due to variations of temperature the fat- liquors sneezed inside and spew formation occurs, and appears as a white spots on the surface of the leather shoes.

By using a inferior quality of preservative in tanning, post- tanning and finishing operations, the bacterial growth start and the whiteness appears on shoe upper during the long storage.

BURNISHING BLEEDS-

During the manufacturing of burnished leather, a burnishing wax is apply on the surface of leather/ shoe with the help of sea sponge or rotator rolling machine. If the application of burnishing wax is not even on the surface of the leather/ shoe, it provide the bleeds and reduce the appearance and beauty of the product. In this process a right application and right pressure is applicable to reduce the burnishing bleeds.

IF THE SHOE AFTER FINISHING IS NOT HAVING SUFFICIENT GLOSS-

The causes are as follows-

1- Excess deposition of cleaners on shoe surface.

2- Sea sponge not properly cleaned and cleaners deposition is uneven.

3- After cleaning the shoes are not well dry.

4- Some moistures are still present inside the leather/ shoe fibers.
5- Without proper drying apply cream on the surface of the shoe.
6- Not proper checking of moisture before application of dressing.
7- It is better to use solvent base dressing in place of water base.
8- In finishing operation, proper care should be taken otherwise thumb impressions visible on finished shoes.
9- In top coat applications, always make thin film because thick film provide dull shining.

FUNGUS APPEARS ON LEATHER SHOES-

In leather manufacturing process, each and every operation the tanners used anti bacterial preservatives (PCP) free to reduce the fungal growth. Most of tanners used preservatives in final stage, so the preservatives deposited on the surface of the leather and it will not penetrate inside the leather fiber. Hence, it is better for tanners to add preservatives in operation like chrome tanning bath, dyeing and fat- liquoring bath, and every seasons preparation in finishing operation. In this way the preservatives penetrate inside the fiber and it will preserve the leather for a long time storage. Similarly in shoe finishing operation, when finishers use cleaners, creams, waxes the addition of PCP free anti fungal preservative is essential, so that we store the shoe for a long period without appearing fungus.

SPRAY MACHINE-

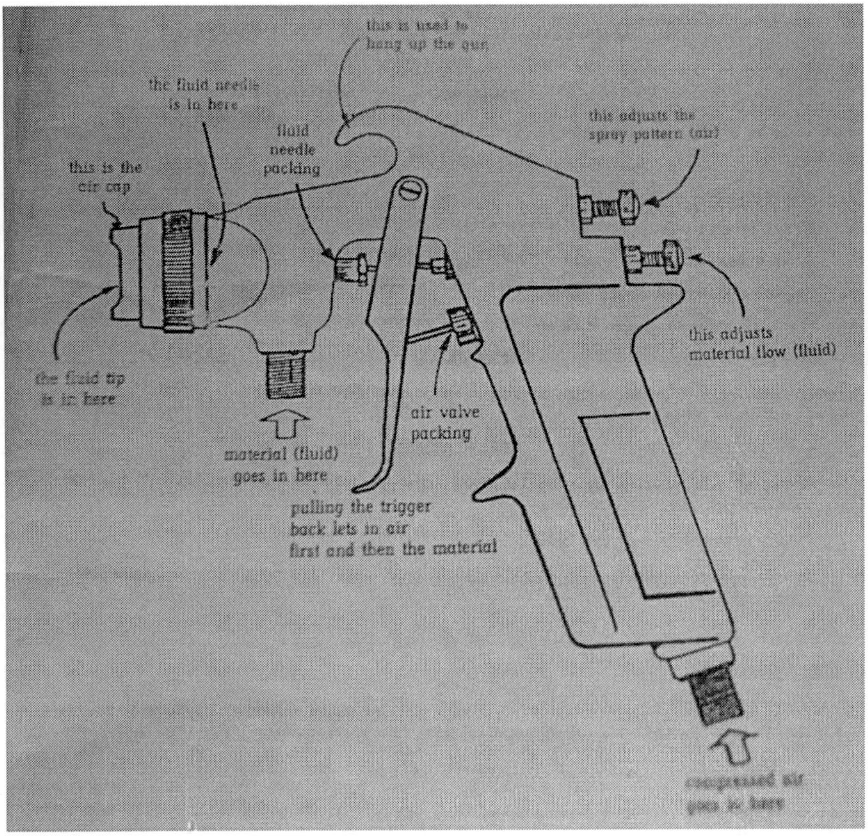

Spray gun is used to deposition of a required amount of seasons on the top surface of the shoes to increase the appearance and beauty of the final products. On most spray guns for top spraying, the following adjustment are required.

1- Adjust material flow by the screw that controls how much liquid is being sprayed when trigger is fully pressed.

2- Adjust the spray patterns-

   a) The shape of the spray patterns on some guns can be altered between round and oval.

   b) " **PEAR DROP" and "BANANA"** shape are incorrect and likely to lead to un-even coverage.

Air pressure is not controlled on gun.

3- Take care of the spray pattern position. This is important on oval spray patterns, which should be vertical.

4- Adjust proper air pressure. Air pressure is not controlled on the gun, but usually on an air pressure controller somewhere near.

The quality depends on-

1- The supply of clean, compressed air.

2- Selection of suitable guns, nozzle sizes and air caps.

3- Good maintenance of the equipment.

4- Adequate extraction of the fume generated during spraying.

5- Spraying method.

Compressed Air-

Air line can be become contaminated with oil or water and the compressor must be drained daily.

Spray booths- It must be adequate size and should be fitted with a flame proof motor.

MAINTENANCE OF SPRAY GUN-

Correct cleaning of the gun will give the following result-

1- It provides trouble free running. At the end of the day clean the gun and cup with water or spirit such as acetone.

2- Never totally immerse the spray gun with spirit, because it can damage the packing.

3- Oil the needle and air valve daily.

4- Clean air and fluid holes with compressed air, **never use wire.**

APPLICATION PROCEDURE-

1- Use good quality sponges and clean the same with water before and after application.

2- For cleaning the shoes use clean cotton cloth and change the cotton cloth regularly.

3- Always allow sometime (5 minutes) for drying all water based products, in between each operations.

4- Before and after spraying water based products, clean the gun with water only.

5- Solvent based products to be sprayed at less pressure (45 psi).

6- Before and after spraying solvent based products, clean the gun with solvents thinner or acetone only.

7- Water based products at more pressure (60- 70 psi).

8- For safety measure, clean the surface of the shoes after application of abrasive and before applying the top dressing.

9- The distance between the shoe and spray gun should be 12 inches.

10- Air pressure in the gun should be in between 2.8 – 3.5 bar.

MACHINE OPERATION INSTRUCTIONS-

1- Switch off the machine when not in use.

2- Operators are required to tie their wearing cloths of similar loose parts of their dress at their back.

3- Do not work more than one person on the machine at a time in one place.

4- Wear the mask while on working on the machine.

5- Clean the machine thoroughly every day.

6- Do not wear loose sleeved garments as the sleeves may become caught while operating the machine, wear tight cloth on overall when you are working.

SPRAY GUN TROUBLE AND REMEDIES-

PATTERNS	CAUSES OF DEFECTIVE SPRAY PATTERNS	REMEDIES
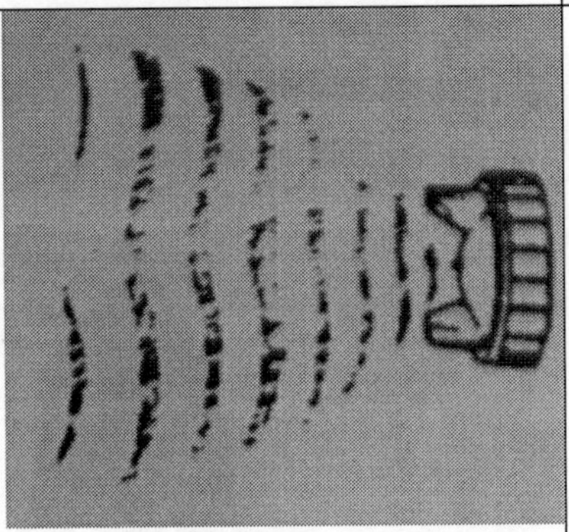	**This problem is caused by air entering the fluid supply- some of the possible causes are-** 1- Lack of material in the container. 2- Tipping spray gun at an excessive angle. 3- Obstructed fluid passage way. 4- Cracked or loose tube in container. 5- Dry or loose fluid needle packing. 6- Fluid tube resting on bottom of	Check all fittings and connections are tight. Check needle packing nut- lubricate packing and retighten packing nut. ---Do not over tighten or needle will jam open when trigger is pulled back. Remove the air and fluid nozzles, clean the nozzles and where nozzle seats into gun.

	cup. 7- Loose fluid nozzle. 8- Material too thick for suction gun. 9- Blocked air vent in container lid.	Release and tighten fluid nozzle using gun spanner.
	1- Heavy right side pattern. 2- Heavy left side pattern.	1- (a) Right side horn holes partially blocked. (b) Dirt or dried paint on right side of fluid tip. **Remedy—** 2- (a) Left side horn holes partia

	Top heavy or bottom heavy pattern. (A)-Horn hole being partially blocked. (B)- Dirt and dried material on the outside of fluid tip. (C) A loose air cap-damaged fluid nozzle or needle.	lly block ed. (b) Dirt on left side of fluid tip. **Remedy-** Clean carefully. Clean and check the air cap is tight. Check needle tip and fluid nozzle for damage. Check for fine

		burr on edge or fluid tip (remove with 600 wet or dry paper).
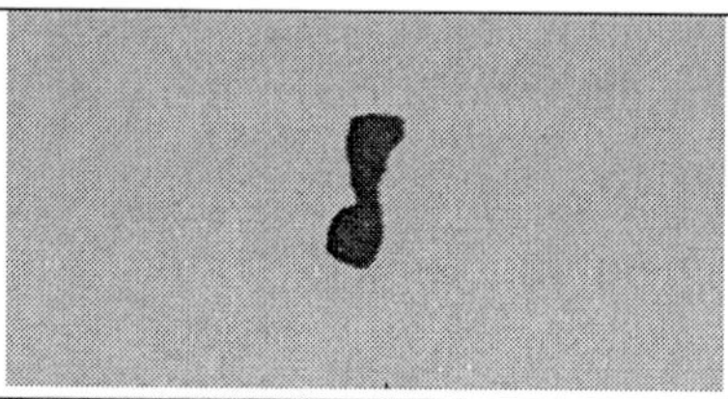	Split pattern. Air pressure too high.	**Reduce pressure.**
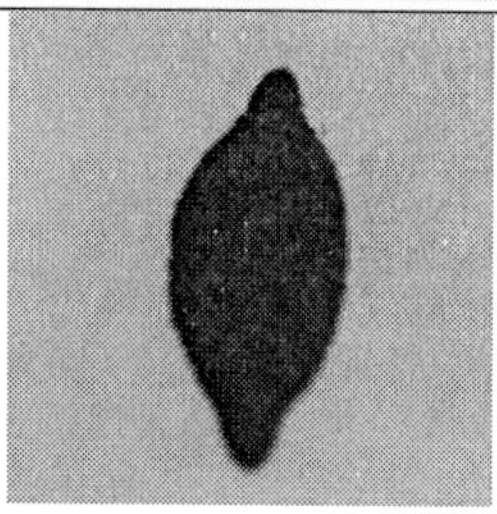	Heavy centre pattern. 1- Atomizing pressure too low. 2- Material too thick. 3- Spreader adjustment valve setting too low. 4- In pressure feed guns the fluid feed pressure may be too high for the atomizing air pressure.	**Increase air pressure.** Balance air and fluid pressure. Open spreader adjustment valve. Check viscosity of material.

THE DONOT AND DO OF SPRAY GUN MAINTENANCE-

DO NOT	DO
1- Place the entire gun in solvent. The solvent will ruin packing and seals in the gun and allow sludge to build in the airways.	CLEAN GUN IMMEDIATELY AFTER USE.
2- Lay the gun on its side before cleaning- Paint will flow back and get into the air passages.	FREQUENTLY OIL THE NEEDLE PACKINGS.
3- Use pliers or multi- grips to dismantle gun.	USE PROPER GUN SPANNER WHEN WORKING ON SPRAY GUN.

SPRAYING TECHNIQUE-

A technique should be developed to obtain an overall even coat of the dressing, without streaks, runs, misted or rough finish. The following are some factors that are important.

1- CHECK SPRAY PATTERN-

The spray pattern should be checked by momentarily spraying on a piece of waste material such as cardboard held squire to the gun. Uneven patterns are usually due to obstructions or damage at the fluid tip.

2- Check air pressure to the gun.

This should be **2.8 to 3.5 Bar (40 -50 psi).**

3- Hold the shoe

---- For shoes and some boots, putting the hand inside is best. The hand is used to present the shoe at the correct angle (not to move it past the gun). The hand will protect the inside of the shoe from over-spray.

---- A glove should be worn for protection.

---- By holding the shoe on the top of the heel may result in leaving marks on successive shoes from the accumulation of spray on the thumb and fingers. The shielding effect of finger and thumb can also leave noticeable areas not sprayed on the side of the heel.

4- Have correct altitude, and distance of the gun from the shoe. The nozzle of the gun should be kept square to the upper surface, at a distance of 30 cm or 12 inches. The fluid flow should be adjusted to give sufficient dressing to "**wet out**" without causing runs.

5- **Spray the shoe**- A typical method of spraying to cover the shoe.

The best method may be to start at the toe, move along the feather edge, up the back seam, along the top- line , over the instep, along the other side top line, down the back seam, along the feather to the toe, and up the centre of the vamp to the top of the quarters (see diagrams).

6-ENSURE DRYING-

Once spraying in completed, very great care must be taken to avoid

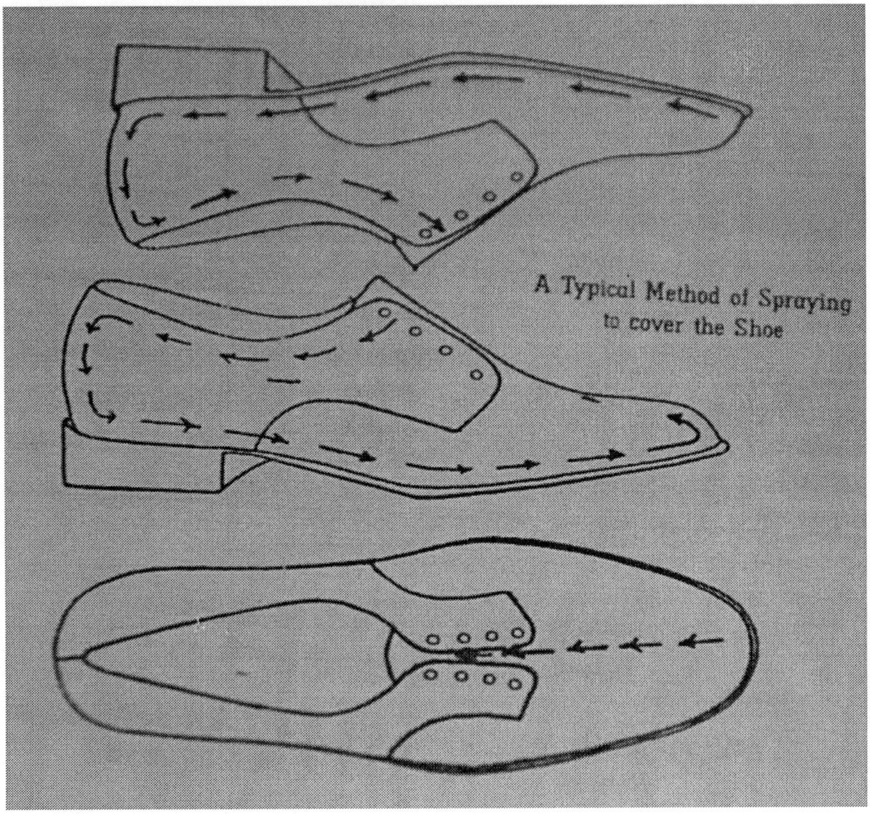

touching the wet surface, or allow anything to contact it until it is thoroughly dry.

FAULTS THAT OCCUR IN SPRAYING-

Types of fault	POSSIBLE CAUSE
Mist of fog	Dressing is too thin. Air pressure too high. Gun held too far away.
Uneven finish (orange peel effect)	Poor cleaning. Wrong air pressure. Wrong gun distance. Unsuitable thinners used. Contaminated dressing. Air hose-contamination.
Rough finish	Insufficient fluid feed. Gun too far away. Too high a spraying pressure.
Streaks	Uneven spray pattern. Gun not square to surface.
Runs or snags	Dressing too thin. Too much dressing applied. Gun not square to work. Working too slowly over the surface.
Splatter on starting	Air valve activator wrongly adjusted. Broken needle spring. Foreign body in fluid tip.
Air leakage from gun	Dirty valve seat. Worn valve seat.

Fluid leakage	Broken spring. Lack of lubrication on valve stem. Worn or damaged fluid tip/ needle. Dirty fluid tip. Wrong size needle.

FINISHING MACHINE-

LONG BOOT IRONING MACHINE-

This machine is very useful to remove the wrinkles of ladies and gents shoes. A aluminum roller is used to remove the wrinkle with the help of a heating devices. It is a well equipped machine and useful for ladies shoes, gentlemen shoes, ironing leather, boot ironing having aluminum molds, heating device, ironing long boots and pedant switch.

1- This machine equips with heating device.
2- The aluminum mold is separated to upper and lower parts. They expands long boots.
3- The aluminum mold can be rotated 180 degree. It is for the convenience of ironing long boots.
4- A pedant switch is equipped in the machine for easy operations.

SPECIFICATIONS-

Item model = **TS- 987 B**
Machine size = **98* 70* 150 cm**
Net Weight = **200 kg**
Power applied = **600 w**

FEATURES-

1- It is automatic machine saves man power and increase efficiency.
2- Electric counter device to control weight for easy replacement.
3- Simple structure for easy maintenance and operations.
4- Low breakdown rate, high machinery life- span.
5- High revolving speed results in large production. Compact machine size contribute to factory space saving.
6- Two styles of aluminum molds can be loaded simultaneously. This machine equips with heating device.
7- The aluminum mold is separated to upper and lower parts. They expands long boots.

CHARACTERISTICS-

1- Long boot ironing machine is a two station forming machine with heated metal lasts suitable for long boot.
2- Each station is equipped with an independent regulators to adjust the stretching of uppers according to the type and number of the uppers.
3- Each last is equipped with a separate mini-safety switch protecting each resistance independently.

HAND IRON-

Hand iron is a automatic ironer. It is used in footwear and garments industry to remove the wrinkles and fold marks. It is used to improve the quality and producing the shining of apparel and allied products. Generally we use only two types of hand iron in the footwear industry.

1- Steam iron

2- Electric iron

Generally the quality of footwear and garments is measured in three characteristics-

1- Durability
2- Utility
3- Emotional appeal

With respect to the raw material used, the product design and the construction of the product. Durability factors are tensile strength, tear strength, abrasive resistance, color fastness and cracking and bursting strength. Utility factors are air permeability, water permeability, thermal conductivity, crease retention, wrinkle resistance, shrinkage and soil resistance. Appeal factors are eye appeal of fabric or leather/ leather garments face, tactile response to the fabric surface, fabric hand (reaction to hand manipulation of the fabric) and eye appeal of the leather garments face, design and drape. The principles involved are the same whether the garments is made of leather, plastic, foam or textile such as woven, knit or felt fabric. In addition to all basic functions, this ironer is fitted with a speed control in order to adjust the right working speed. Finally, it has two temperature selectors, that can be used separately, from each other to iron smaller articles (energy- saving). It is recommended for home application with higher requirements.

DESIGN-

1- Folding storage system.
2- Ideal standard length.
3- Free end of the roller, iron cylindrically shaped articles easily.
4- Free wheeling of the roller enable to guide the laundry under the shoe after laying it under the roller.
5- The ironing machine is fitted with casters for easy transportation.

OPERATIONS-

1- The operation done carefully that the final product should be crease free.

2- Always maintain required temperature otherwise the coloring material will burn and damage the required gloss.

3- If wrinkle is more then apply Teflon paper on the shoe surface.

TOP LINE FORMING MACHINE-

This machine is applicable to final molding and finishing, before removed and packed, melt the glue of the heel deformed with electric heating and then cool it down for molding. The heel after molding will have a straight and perfect shape. In addition, the heating and cooling will remove the damp so as to keep it from mold growth.

Free regulated temperature and heating time upon the material of vamp. Time can be adjusted when the temperature reaches 150 degree c. It has a good molding effect.

SPECIFICATIONS-

Dimension (L * W *H)	=	**700 * 620 * 1250 MM**
Net weight	=	**185 kg**
Power	=	**0.75 kW**
Voltage	=	**220 V / Hz**
Production	=	**1400 pairs/ 8 hrs.**

EXAMPLES OF FINISHING PROCEDURES FOR DIFFERENT TYPES OF LEATHER-

1- FULL GRAIN CALF LEATHER- ANILINE AND SEMI-ANILINE-

The characteristics of these leather is the color transparency and brightness. The leather that has not received any coating of pigmented finish. So that the original grain surface can be seen through the finish completely unhindered by any pigment particles.

Semi- aniline leather is defined by-**"leather which has been aniline dyed or stained, incorporating a small quantity of pigment, not so much as to conceal the natural characteristics of the hide".** For finishing of this type of leather some of the important systems are-

1- **Clean the shoes** (It should be free from dirt, oils and any contaminants).

Apply the sealing cream dry well and put a small quantity of abrasive wax on a cotton brush and then brush it at a medium speed. Polish it with a woolen brush treated with carnauba wax.

2- BRUSH- OFF LEATHER-

The characteristics of these leathers is that gives a two tone effect on brushing on a cotton brush.

FOR NATURAL GLOSS-

First of all clean the shoes properly

Once dry, brush on cotton brush at 700 – 800 rpm with the addition of abrasive wax.

Again clean the shoes.

Apply a suitable cream (as per requirement).

Once dry, brush on a cotton brush at 700 – 800 rpm with abrasive wax.

Polish it with a woolen brush treated with carnauba wax 700 -800 rpm.

FOR HIGH GLOSS-

Clean the shoes-

Once dry, brush on a cotton brush at 700- 800 rpm with abrasive wax.

Clean the shoe.

Apply a suitable filler (may be sealing cream/ liquid)

Once dry, apply a suitable top coat.

Polish it with a woolen brush treated with carnauba wax.

FOR VERY HIGH GLOSS-

Clean the shoe.

Once dry, brush on cotton brush at 700 – 800 rpm with abrasive wax.

Clean the shoe.

Apply a high shine top dressing, one or two coat as per the requirement.

Polish it with a woolen brush treated with carnauba wax.

SHOE BOTTOM FINISHING

The type of finish on a shoe bottom is partly a matter of taste but sometimes it is influenced by the style of shoe, color of shoe and quality of materials. It is considered in special circumstances to hide the natural appearance of the leather. So that even though leather varies considerably in quality. Some attempts are made to restrict the degree of appearance by using bottom finish which contains a limited amount of cover or body (pigment).

In order of quality of soles, the following finishes are suggested-

- **A) NATURAL GUM FINISH**
- **B) TRANSPARENT GUM STAIN**
- **C) DAMP DOWN**
- **D) PIGMENTED GUM**

E) SILICO TYPES

F) PAINTS

A) **NATURAL GUM FINISH-**

The use of gum transacanth mucilage only put a thin film of gum over the grain and does not change the color in any way. When faked polished the true characteristics of the leather are enhanced.

B) **TRANSPARENT GUM STAINS-**

With an addition of a dye such as to give the desired color. Leather colors are most common.

C) **DAMP DOWN-** This finish does not contain some pigment but in such a small quantity that the surface is not covered. The usual ingredients are – Epsom salt, oxalic acid, gum transacanth, bottom balls and distilled water. The finish must be kept in suspension by periodic shaking or stirring and when applied by the flannel, it damps the sole but on drying leaves the deposit of gum and chalk. This surface can be finally faked and polished or finished with French chalk.

This finish is often used on the fore part in conjunction with black or brown burnished waist.

D) **PIGMENTED GUM-** This finish is the substitute for the natural and transparent finish and basically a gum polish. The addition of pigment and a little binder (casin) retains a thin layer of pigment enough. To cover minor defects but not enough to give a painted effect. The method of application by sponge or in some cases by flat hair brush but always the surplus laying on top each brushed of immediately by brushing.

E) **SILICO TYPE-** This type of finish is similar to paint in method of application i.e. brushed with a camel hair brush and allowed to dry. The silico is method on a high speed rag nap which is a changed periodically by the operative with a friction wax (abrasive properties) which is turn cuts down the deposit of paint on a surface giving some slight degree of transparency.

F) **PAINTS-** This type of brush applied finish may used for two reasons-

1- For uniformity For covering the surface of inferior leather

The use of paint on some ladies shoes especially Louis heel is a good example of the use of paint for uniformity. The type of finish which good constitute a suitable paint is one which covers the surface does not peel flake or crack.

It is important to work cleanly the paint is difficult to be removed when dry. The brush should be wide enough to almost cover the waist 1" – 2" brushes being normal.

The color usually used are a variation of the leather colors but paints are obtainable. The consistency of the paint should be thin enough to allow the brush marks to disappear leaving a smooth surface. Frequent stirring is necessary to avoid thickening.

The damp down is applied on a flannel pad rubbed in which a circular motion and the excess is wiped off in the length direction with second pad. If the waist is of different color the brushing ink is applied on a camel hair brush from the joint to the breast of heel and the top piece. When the waist finish is dry, fake should be smeared on the forepart to keep it clean. Any black wax will be deposited on the fake can be rubbed off easily.

CLEANING-

Traditionally this is a hand operation and will employ various solvents and cleaners to remove all kinds of dirt, stains etc. found on finish shoes. The method will vary to extent according to the type of dirt like sometimes a cloth pad is more efficient than a sponge. It is customary to clean all shoes whether they need or not. Whatever method is used a trial should be made with a new leather. This trial should be made under typical factory conditions where possible.

(a) **CELLULOSE FINISHED LEATHER- Cellulose** finished leather is confined generally to goat and sheep used for the slipper trade. The cellulose is water proof and will be easily cleaned with soapy water. Any solvent for cellulose such as a acetone should be avoided.

(b) **PATENT- Whether** calf or goat can be treated with cellulose.

(c) **PIGMENT**- Finished sides and calf may cause the greatest trouble in cleaning owing to the lack of fastness which spoil the surface when water is used in cleaning. To avoid this, it is better to clean dry by brushing but extreme causes may be cleaned with petrol.

(d) **PLASTIC (SYNTHETIC RESIN)**- Finished calf and sides are fast and will usually be cleaned with a general cleaner which consists of-

1- Water
2- Soap
3- Methylated spirit
4- Methyl acetate
5- Ammonia
6- Sassafras oil
7- Citronella oil

The various constituents of the cleaners will act separately such that mythil will dissolve wax and ammonia will soften greases and oil.

(e)-SUEDE LEATHER- This leather is the most difficult to clean and great effort should be made to keep it clean. Generally an abrasive paper is used to clean the oil stains but covers are also used to prevent the suede from picking up dirt and stains.

FILLERS- Filler is sprayed orb applied by sponge to give a coat and forms a base to take the upper dressing. It also covers the opening.

DRESSING- Dressing is applied on the shoe to restore the original Appearance of upper and also give a brighter and shiny look.

CLASSIFICATION OF DRESSINGS-

1- Shellac dressing
2- Split and kip dressing
3- Case in dressing
4- Calf dressing
5- Spirit dressing
6- Cellulose dressing
7- Synthetic dressing
8- Suede dressing
9- Dubbing dressing

1- **SHELLAC-** Shellac mixes easily in water when an alkali is present. Borax is commonly used for its innocuous effect on leather. The amount of circulations of shellac in many formula with influence the luster. Both black and brown dressings can be produced from TN orange flake shellac together with other ingredients such as ammonia soap, oil and gum soften the film. Shellac alone produces a hard, brittle film and needs the addition of soap, oil and gum to improve the plasticity.

The dressing has never been popular for high grade shoes and today is only found on footwear such as boys and girls kip or side footwear and cheap shoes. Generally, the finish is inclined to be gaudy and gives good shoes a cheap appearance. It is usually applied with a sponge.

2-CASIN- It can replace the shellac in dressings. (it is also ingredient of willow calf dressing). It is also used in consumption with shellac and is readily soluble in water with borax or ammonia. It is cheaper than shellac but the luster is not so great.

3-SPLIT AND KIP- These dressing are combined to the particular production of heavy field boots. It consists of heavy concentration of skin glue, soap, oil, grease and wax together with dies to form a slow dyeing viscous liquid. To distinct types of dressing are used.

1- Bright
2- Dull

The group (1) contain in addition to some of the materials already maintain casein and shellac to give luster. Group (2) will have grease, tallow, wax and shellac. In cold weather, there is always a danger with this dressing to spew.

4-CALF DRESSING- It is desirable when dressing a calf to retain as much of the natural feel of the leather as possible consequently the film must blend with the leather reacting to every movement perfectly. One such dressing can be achieved from wax made in to liquid from by suitable solvent. This liquid wax dressing can be sponge applied to form an extremely this fill. An alternative form of dressing can be of water soap and wax. Wax turpentine pastes such as are in common use for shoe polishing can also be used. Where some color is required this can be included in any of these types.

5-SPIRIT DRESSING- These are seldom use for normal production unless the material has proved vary liable to spew this is generally used on shoes which are stripped to avoid spewing during the cold.

One of the most common uses of spirit dressing is for window shoes to enhance the luster for display purposes. This dressing can only be successfully applied by camel hair brush and one thin coat at a time, two or more coats will produce a brilliant luster and totally prevent spewing.

6-CELLULOSE DRESSING- The transparent cellulose spray dressing in the little demand in shoe industry making outdoor footwear owing to the difficulty obtaining a film which will not flake or crack in wear. It is important to remove all grease from the surface before spraying.

Cellulose has the same defect as any other film forming substances as much as it quickly cracks when bent. This defect has made it unsuitable for shoes although recently new plasticizers have been added which reduce this tendency.

7-SYNTHETIC RESIN- These have in recent year proved popular in the manufacture of medium to good quality men and women with leather finish with synthetic resin.

The virtues are this type of dressing are-

1- Closed bond with the leather
2- Thickness of the film
3- Complete flexibility
4- Transparency in film
5- Tackiness when wet producing less rebound while spraying
6- Absence of particles reduces risk of clogging spray gun to a negligible factor.

When spraying, care must be taken to use regular pressure of 50 lbs. to ensure an even application. The distance of the gun from the shoe should be 12 inches approx. and the shoe should be moved sufficiently fast to avoid runs.

8-SUEDE- Suede can be treated in two ways either by power of the same shade and borax in that condition are by power and find transparent spray by spray only. The power method is objected because of the likelihood of its coming into contact with the cloth of the customers.

Spray must be fine and not to contusive. The spray will not unify varying colors but will enhance the appearance and also will fix almost entirely the power, the use of spray only will be sufficient on shoes, which has been covered adequately during process.

9-DUBBIN DRESSING- Curried leather can be used to clean the surface dirt and subsequently treated with combination of various oil and greases to restore the heavy grease effect.

BOTTOM FINISHING MACHINE-

TOP SOLE BUFFING-

Purpose- Top soles are buffed to remove minor surface marks which will allow the color to penetrate well and to achieved and uniform finish. Buffing is done from toe to waist at first and then from heel to waist.

HINTS- Over buffing should not be done which will never give a good finish.

- **Buffing should be done carefully.**
- Edge of the top sole should not be damaged.
- Sand paper of proper grid must be used.
- Buffing should never be done on wet leather surface.

MATERIAL-

Silicon carborandum (80 – 100) grid 4 inch wide.

EDGE AND HEEL TRIMMING-

Purpose- Edge trimming is done to make the two ends of the pair equal in shape and size and to produce the required shape on the edge. It is also done to repair a uniform base for edge setting and finish.

Operation-

1- After adjusting the cutter as per thickness of the edge the trimming start from the waist and ends on the other side of the waist.

2- After the edge is being trimmed the cutter is adjusted as per the thickness of the heel and trimmed as under. Trimming start from the waist and goes round the heel and ends on the other side of the waist.

HINTS-

1- Pairs to be checked for correct shape cutting.
2- Trimming is done while the soles are dry.
3- Cutter should be properly adjusted.
4- Top sole should always be held against the shield are ring for obtaining correct shape.
5- Edge should be held square and in a right angle against the cutter.
6- Trimming should be done smoothly to gain the shape of sole.
7- Trimming should be done always in pairs.
8- After trimming pair must be checked for accuracy in shape and size.
9- Cutter should be sharpened correctly while needed.
10- Trimming should never be done on blunt cutters.

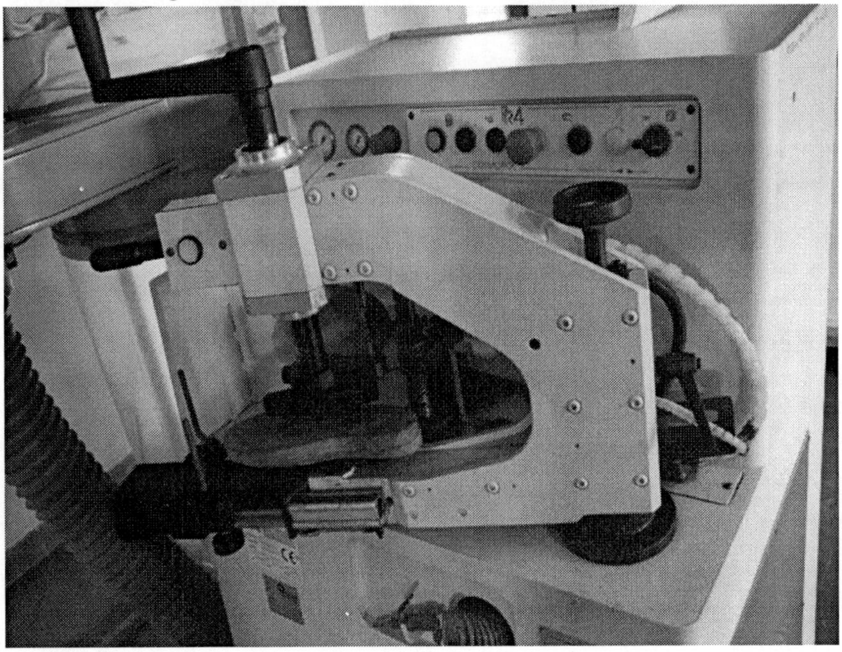

EDGE SETTING-

Purpose- To cover the joining line between top sole and bottom sole, which is found after trimming and also to set the edge so that shape of the edge will be retained for a long time.

OPERATION-

1- Edge is damp with a moist cloth.
2- Iron of correct thickness as per the thickness of the edge is chosen.
3- Edge of the sole and heel is pressed against the rotating iron uniformly.

HINTS-

1- Edge is to be damped properly.
2- Selection of iron must be correct.
3- Should be pressed evently and uniformly.
4- Edge should not be tipped on one side, it should be held square against the iron.

BUFFING OF THE EDGE-

Purpose- To open the fibres which will allow the color to penetrate well.

OPERATION-

Edge of the sole and heel is buffed uniformly with a piece of sand paper slightly (grit 8- -100).

HINTS-

1- Sand paper of correct grit must be used.
2- Buffing should be done carefully without spoiling the shape of the edge.
3- Edge must be dry while buffing.

SHAPING OF THE HEEL BREAST-

Purpose- Shaping and evening up of the surface of the heel front are done to obtain an appearance that the heel is built in one block and for better appearance.

OPERATION-

1- The uneven edge of the heel front is trimmed with a shoe maker's knife.

2- The surface of the edge is then buffed with a small piece of sand paper (80- 180) grit.

3-

HINTS-

1- Care must be taken that the sole is not cut.

2- Shape of the heel front should not be damaged.

3- Cutting should be straight and no undercut.

4- Heel front should be at 90 degree to the sole.

5- Cutting should be even.

6- Knife must be sharp not blunt.

7- Sand paper of correct grit to be used.

EDGE COLORING-

Purpose- To decorate the edge and to cover minor manufacturing defects.

OPERATION- Color is applied evently round the edge of sole and heel with a brush with soft bristle.

HINTS-

1- Care must be taken not to damage the top sole and bottom sole with color.

2- Hand should be kept clean during this operation.

3- Brush and containers should be kept clean.

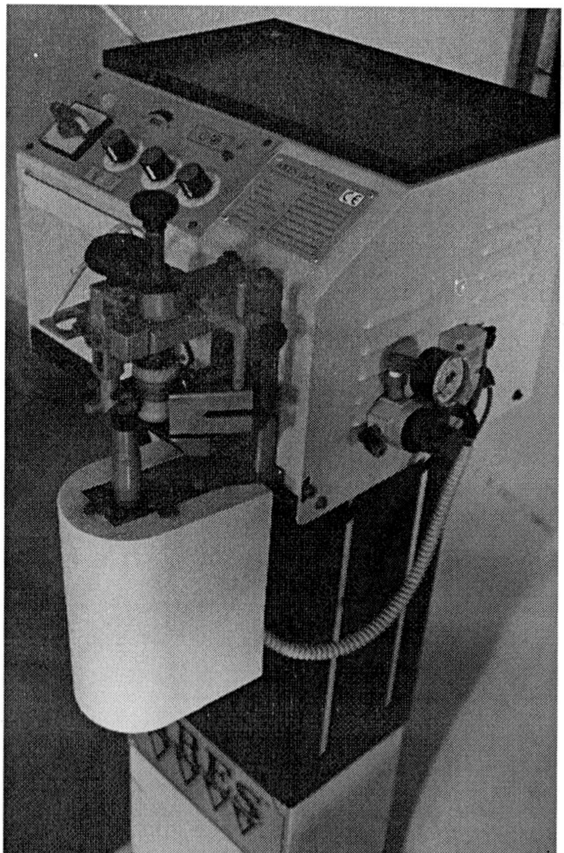

TOP SOLE COLORING-

Purpose- Decoration and sometimes minor defects of top sole are covered.

OPERATION- Color is applied on the top sole evently and uniformly with a hair brush with long bristle.

MATERIAL- Generally, color of the same shade as upper as used. Sometimes color of contrasting combination shade is also used.

HINTS-

1- Care must be taken not to damage the top sole and bottom sole with color.

2- Hand should be kept clean during this operation.

3- Brush and container should be kept clean.

SECOND EDGE SETTING-

Purpose-

1- To retain the shape of edge for a long time.

2- To make the edge water repellant.

3- To make the edge attractive.

OPERATION- Melted wax is applied lightly on the edge and then the edge is set against the stop iron.

HINTS-

1- Wax should be applied lightly.

2- While setting the edge, wax should penetrate inside and not stay at the top.

BOTTOM SCOURING-

Purpose- To remove the hyaline layer of the sole and to achieve and uniform even and smooth surface, which will take a uniform bottom finish.

OPERATION-

1- Sole is buffed in circular motion.

2- Buffing start from the edge and gradually goes towards the center.

3- Top piece is buffed on the roller at the first.

HINTS-

1- Sand paper of proper grit to be used.

2- Should not be over buffed which will damage the sole or even burn the leather which will be very difficult or impossible to be finished.

3- While buffing the waist or shank, care must be taken not to damage the heel front.

4- It should never be tried to buff with an old used sand paper which is not in position to buff any more.

5- Buffing should always done while the sole is dry.

MATERIAL- Abrasive silicon carborandum

Grit no- 80- 100 for rough

Grit no- 120- 150 for fine.

BOTTOM MAKING-

Purpose- Bottom is finished for decoration purpose and at the same time a little wax is applied to make the surface a little water repellant. For inferior leather the defects can be covered with pigment or dies.

Bottom can be finished in many ways such as-

1- Transparent gum finish
2- Natural finish
3- Pigment or dye finish
4- Dope finish

Natural finish is only applied on soles of very good leather where soles are used from inferior leather a pigment or dye may be used to cover the defects.

NATURAL FINISH-

OPERATION- 1- **After** buffing, the dust must be removed totally.

2-Bottom finishes then applied with a clean fine hair brush or a rag uniformly and evenly in a circular motion on the soles and top pieces.

3-The soles are than kept in a place till finish gets dry.

4-When the finish is dry the soles are polished against the finish brush on which a little wax is applied to obtain a glazed finish.

HINTS-

1- Finish must be applied uniformly and evenly.

2- Brushing should be done with a very light pressure.

3- Heavy pressure will only darken the finish.

4- If the finish comes on the edge that should be wiped off.

5- Brushing should be done in a swift movement.

REMARKS- If stains are formed on the soles than they may be cleaned after buffing with a very week oxalic acid solution to obtain a better finish.

TOP SOLE POLISHING

PURPOSE- To obtain a glazed surface.

OPERATION- Natural or any suitable wax apply on the same shade on the brush and than the top soles are polished in the same way as bottom polishing.

HINTS- It is similar to bottom polishing, the edge is brushed in the same way and for the same purpose.

TOP SOLE MAKING

PURPOSE- This is only done to decorate the top sole to make it attractive.

OPERATION- A special device like a divider is used for making 2 to 3 lines are drawn equidistance from the edge all along the sole and heel. One leg of the device runs against the edge being guided by the edge of the sole and heel and the other leg which has a sharp folded edge marks the lines.

HINTS-

1- Line must be uniform all round and they must be equidistant all along.
2- Line must be marked very carefully otherwise in place of making it attractive it will only make it ugly.
3- Line must not very deep.

FITTING OF UPPER-

PURPOSE- The upper are the fitted at their correct position to the bottom to make the complete shoes.

OPERATION-

1- The straps ends are skived to avoid bulge on the top sole.
2- The slots are opened with a screw driver.
3- The straps are inserted into the slots.
4- A piece of leather with a slot at the end is used to hold the rivets firmly and conveniently on their position and then they are driven in with a hammer.

HINTS-

1- The straps ends are skived to avoid bulge on the top sole.

2- The slots are opened with a screw driver.

3- The straps are inserted into the slots.

4- A piece of leather with a slot at the end is used to hold the rivets firmly and conveniently on their position and then they are driven in with a hammer.

HINTS-

1- Straps should not be skived too much.

2- Straps should be inserted up to the marking otherwise it will give an uneven and wrong fitting.

3- Care should be taken while riveting the straps are not damaged.

4- After the straps are fitted, they should be checked for firmness and correct fitting.

Final brushing, grading, checking and boxing. Finally the finish shoes/ chappals are brushed and kept in pairs. Before boxing the following points are to be checked.

1- All operations are done correctly.

2- They tally with job cards regarding lot numbers, sizes and designs. Then they are boxed in pairs and a level is pasted which will give the following information.

   a) Description
   b) Article no.
   c) Size
   d) Job no.
   e) Grade

FINISHING ITEMS-

The finishing items may be required for upper leather, leather soles, leather insole, leather heels, and for upper repairing etc.

The purpose of the shoe finishing is to add value for the customer by improving aesthetic llok of the shoe. Actually finish is what actually gives further value to the material.

There are the following materials used for shoe finishing.

1- Creams
2- Waxes
3- Pigments for repairing
4- Liquids for finishing
5- Cleaner
6- Die for edge coloring

Shoe finishing items can be divided into two parts.

First part is general finishing item those are required for all seasons. Those should be purchased as per projection of new orders.

Second part is specific finishing items those are required in case of bulk orders.

Consumption per pair of shoe finishing products like creams, waxes, repairing crayons per pair is calculated in kg. While items like pigments for finishing, cleaner, die for edge coloring are calculated in liters.

SHOE PACKING SYSTEM (FINISHING)

Packaging is the art, science and technology of enclosed products for distribution, storage, sales and use. Packaging also refers to the process of design, evaluation and production of packages.

THE PURPOSE OF PACKAGING-

1- **PHYSICAL PROTECTION-**

   The objects enclosed in the package may require protection from, among other things, socks, vibration, compression, temperature etc.

2- **BARRIER PROTECTION-**

A barrier from oxygen, water, vapour, dust etc. is often required. Permeation is a critical factor in design. Some packages contains desiccants or oxygen absorbers to help extend self- life. Modified atmospheres or controlled atmospheres are also maintained in shoe packages. Keeping the contents clean, fresh and safe for the intended shelf- life is a primary function.

3- **CONTAINMENT OR AGGLOMERATION-**

Small objects are typically grouped together in one package for reasons of efficiency. For example- a single cartoon of 10 pair shoes require less physical handling than 10 single shoe boxes.

4- **INFORMATION TRANSMISSION-**

Packages and label communicate how to use, transport, recycle or dispose of the package or product with pharmaceuticals, food, medical and chemical products. Some types of information are required by governments. Some packages and labels are also used for track and trace purpose.

5- **MARKETING-**

The packaging and labels can be used by marketers to encourage potential buyers to purchase the product. Package graphic design and physical design have been important and constantly evolving phenomenon for several decades. Marketing communications and graphic design are applied to the surface of the package and (in many cases) the point to sale display.

6- **SECURITY-**

Packaging can play an important role in reducing the security risks of shipments. Packages can be made with improved temper resistance. Packages can be engineered to help to reduce the risks of package pilferage. Some package constructions are more resistant to pilferage and some have pilfer indicating seals. Packages may include authentication seals and use security printing to help indicate that the package and contents are not counter foil. Packages also can include anti- theft devices, such as dye-packs, that can be activated or detected by devices at exit points and require specialized tools to deactivate. Using packaging in this way is a means of loss prevention.

7- **CONVENIENCE-**

Packages can have features that add convenience in distribution, handling, stacking, display, sale, opening, reclose, use, dispensing and reuse.

8- **PORTION CONTROL-**

Single serving or single dosage packaging has a precise amount of contents to control usage. Bulk- commodities (such as salt) can be divided into packages that are a more suitable size for individual households. It is also aids the control of inventory and selling.

PACKAGING TYPES-

1- **PRIMARY PACKAGING (SHOE BOX PACKING)** - It is the material that first envelops the product and holds it. This usually is the smallest units of distribution or use and is the package which is in direct contact with the contents.

2- **SECONDARY PACKAGING- (CARTON PACKING)** - It is the outside the primary packaging perhaps used to group primary packages together.

3- **TERTIARY PACKAGING (CONTAINER PACKING)** - It is used for bulk handling, Warehouse storage and transport shipping. The most common form is a pallatized unit load that packs tightly into containers.

MATERIALS RELATED TO PACKING DEPARTMENT-

FOR SHOE BOX PACKING-

a) **SHOE BOX (INNER BOX)** - This is one of major packaging items. Before bulk ordering of inner box it is very important to determine the perfect dimensions (l * b *h) in centimeters.

For normal gents shoes standard dimensions are 33cm length, 20 cm width and 12.5 cm height.

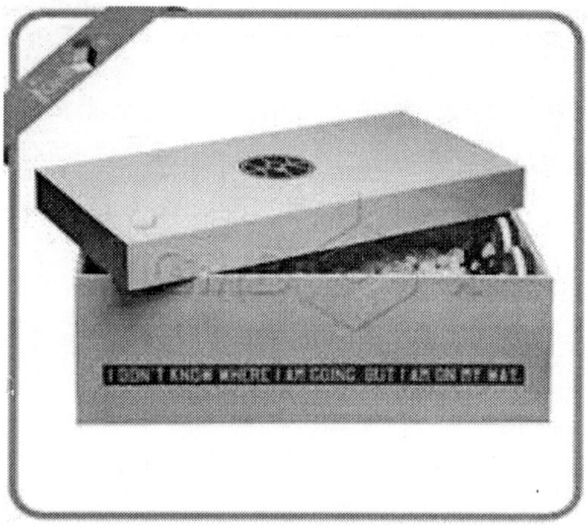

Shoe box should not too much tight or loose.

Biggest size shoe should be taken during inner box dimension checking. If biggest size shoe is not available then add extra length as per standard grading system.

b) **SHOE BOX LABEL**- This is the self – adhesive label pasted on shoe box as per specified by the customer.

Generally the following information may be printed on a shoe box label.

1- Customer Name-

2- Article Number/ Style Name

3- Size

4- Price with barcode

5- Manufacturing Date

6- Article picture

c) **TISSUE PAPERS-** Tissue papers are used for the following purpose-

For stuffing- For this, plain tissue paper of slightly lower grade can be used for stuffing purpose.

For wrapping- For wrapping plain or printed (as per specified by the customer) can be used.

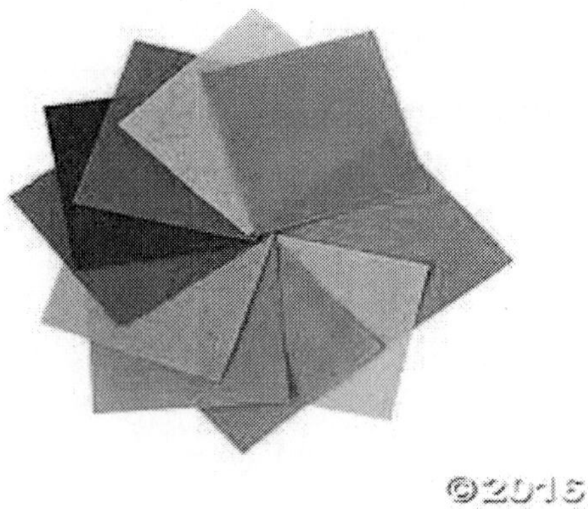

d) **HANG TAG**

It is used as per requirement of the customer. Detail of hang tag should be printed as per specification given in the customers brochure.p

Hang tag may be used as one piece per pair or sometimes attached with the both odds. This is also specified by the customer in their packaging details.

There is a string is also used to hang the hang tag with the shoe. Length of string may be specified by the customer.

c) **Pictogram**- Pictogram is a type of small sticker which shows the material composition of a shoe.

If a leather shoe is made of with the following materials-

Upper - Leather

Lining - Leather

Sole - PU

Then the correct pictogram will show the upper part of leather, lining part of leather and bottom sole as a PU material. If lining material is textile, then in pictogram in place of lining material it will show the textile.

e) **Leaflet- It** is a piece of paper that gives you information or advertises something. It is a specific thing which is asked by very few customers.

It is put in the inner box after final packing.

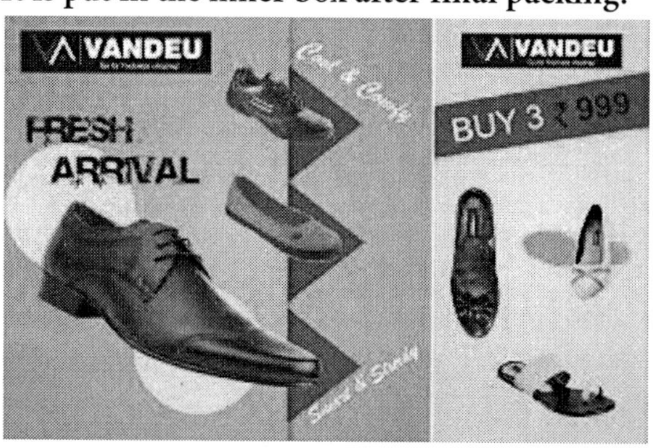

f) **Barcode Labels-**

A bar code (often seen as a single word, barcode) is the small image of lines (bars) and spaces that is affixed to retail store items, identification cards, and postal mail to identify a particular product number, person or location.

During a shopping excursion to a shopping mall, you would have noticed the cashier scanning your products using some laser device to produce a bill. What actually he is doing that he is reading the product barcodes using a Laser/ Barcode scanner. Barcode scanner reads the code, data is sent to the computer, and computer looks up into the database for the price and description of the item.

Barcodes are structured to contain specific product related information. It basically encodes alphanumeric characters and symbols using black and white strips, also called bars. Bar- coding is one of the AIDC (Automatic Identification and Data Collection) technologies which reduce human involvement in data entry and collection and thereby also reducing error and time.

Barcode is a kind of label which may be pasted on sole, hang tags, box label, inner quarter lining or socks lining.

h) - Laces- Laces may be classified on the following basis.

As per shape-

1- Round
2- Flat
3- Oval

As per material-

These are made of natural fibers such as cotton laces etc. Or synthetic fibers such as nylon, textured polyester, spun polyester and polypropylene as well as the traditional natural materials.

--- Nylon may be waxy or non waxy.

--- Cotton may be waxy or non- waxy.

There are very important to determine the correct length of a shoe. There are the following points should be followed during finalizing the length of the lace for the bulk orders.

1- Take the sample and check how many holes or eyelets are given for the lacing.
2- Follow the length as per table.
3- Always remember the length should not too much long or short.
4- When you select the right length then a proper flower will be formed after lacing.

TABLE FOR LACE LENGTH FINALIZATION-

HOLES	Length in cm.	HOLES	Length in cm.
2	45	9	
3	65	10	130
4	75- 85	11	
5	85- 90	12	150
6	100	14	180
7		15	
8	120	16	200

It can help to finalizing the correct length of a shoe.

i) Silica gel anti- mold stickers or micro- pak-

Silica gel is derived from sand and ONLY absorbs moisture. If not enough is used then there is still moisture present and if the sachets are not kept perfectly dry before use they will be ineffective when packed with the shoes. There is also a clear health danger if the silica gel is ingested by workers or customers.

Beware of silica sachets that also contain toxic substances.

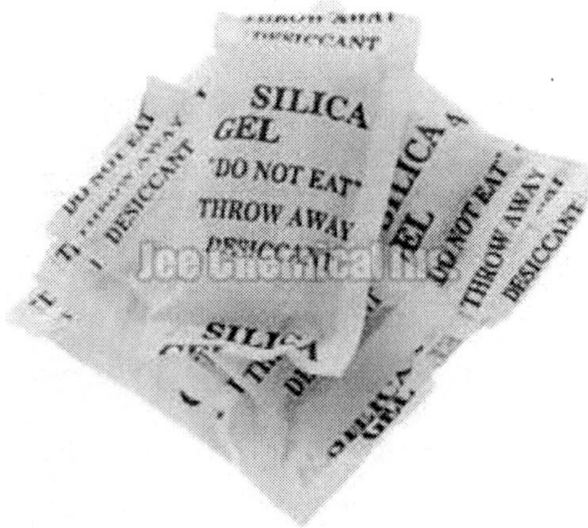

Micro- Pak enhanced packaging stickers are placed in the box at the time of final packing. When humidity is high the moisture in the air enters the sticker and starts a reaction that creates a Micro- Pak atmosphere environment. This Micro- Pak atmosphere environment spreads throughout the package helping to keep the item clean and fresh.

j) **OUTER CARTON-**

Outer carton is made after the finalization of the inner box or shoe box. It may be plain form or printed form.

During finalization of outer carton dimension (l * b * h) always check the **outer limits given in the brochure by the customer. Outer cartons are made.**

1- **Corrugated (Pasted) cartoons-**

This is costly and used for export purpose. All good customers are always preffered for this due to good strength, durability during trandport.

It may be used for 6 pairs, 8 pairs. 10 pairs, 12 pairs etc as per requirement of the customer. In shoe export minimum **7 ply corrugated cartons are used.**

2-Stapled Cartons- This is having less durability and it can be made in lower cost. It is used in domestic shoes packaging during small distance transportations. It can be used during export business.

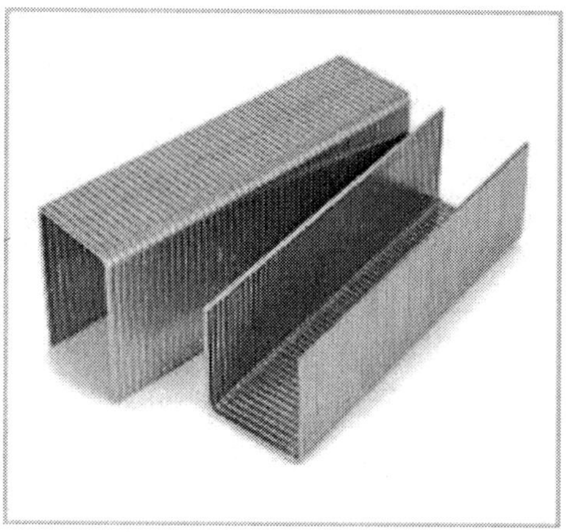

CARTON TAPE- Carton tapes are very important part of packaging. The recommended width of cartoon tape is 3 inches. It may be classified as-

1- Plain Colored
2- Plain transparent
3- Printed transparent
4- Colored printed.

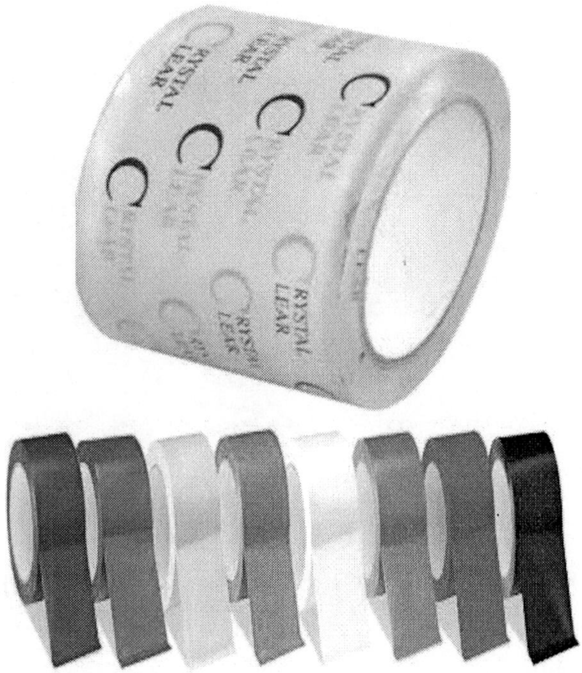

OUTER CARTON LABEL- It is required after final sealing/ packing of inner box into the outer carton. In export business sometimes customer may ask for printed carton or sometimes plain. So requirement of carton labels for shipping marks & side marks are made according to the customers instructions.

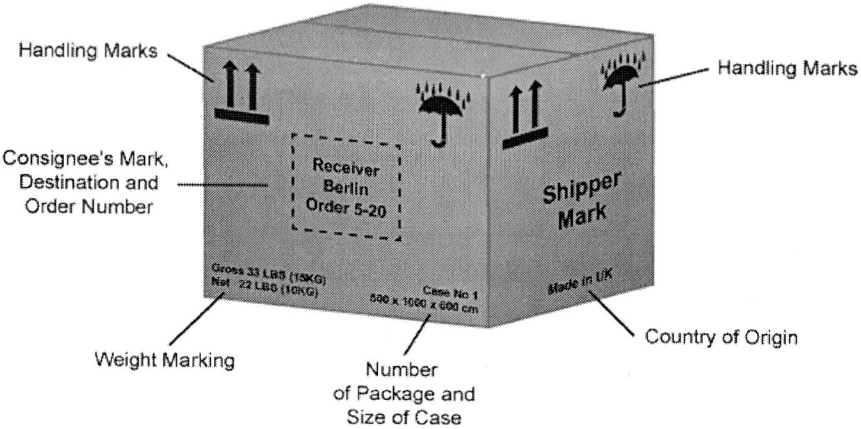

POLYBAG PACKING-

a) **POLY BAG WITH HANGER- Poly bag used printed form- Sometimes** there is a rope or dori is used in the top of poly bag or sometimes they ask for hanger also for hanging display. The size of poly bag should be checked carefully before finalizing the dimensions for bulk order and take approval from the buyer also.

b) **OUTER CARTON WITH CRATE- Carton with crate is used for poly bag packing. Carton dimensions are finalized earlier and crates are made according to the inner dimensions of the carton. Crates are made in such way those can be easily inserted and removed.**

SHOE MAKING TIPS

1- Never use ball pen for stitch marking. These marks can never be erased and will result in claims, use a silver refill/ pen.

2- To check the temperature readings on the heat setter, activator, interlining in ironing press are correct use a digital thermometer (infrared type). This is available for about Rs. 2000 to 3000.

3- For hand punched mocassins always use a divider to mark a line on the apron & vamp, so that all punches are equal distance from the edge.

4- For materials like kid, it is always better to attach interlining & then skived raw edges which are visible on the shoe.

5- Always do edge coloring before stitching. If you color after stitching stains may be caused.

6- When you have non moving leather re-dyeing all into dark brown/ black & use on one order.

7- Excessive halogenation of TPR soles causes weakening of the sole & is not desirable.

8- Always test soles for cold cracking at – 30 degree c, if you are exporting to such countries.

9- Never iron after applying finishing cream. This can cause white streaks which are not removable. If you have to iron, wash the cream with solvent before ironing.

10- While stitching on curves remember that on a concave curve the stitch length will get smaller and on a convex curve it will get bigger. Therefore for 2 row stitching always start from the same end otherwise you will get variation in stitch length.

11- For folded top line do not lock at the end of the seam otherwise the seam may split while folding. Leave 1 cm of thread extra.

12- Use a Ps needle point whenever a high stitch density is required.

13- Endure that the thread guide just before threading is there. (for thread control)

14- The pressure wheel must be as close as possible to the needle. Central to the needle and must rotate freely for correct stitch formation.

15- While stitching French binding pull the binding slightly and have it facing upwards to avoid wrinkles while folding especially on curves.

16- Do not use the same needle plate for a size 70 needle and a size 120 needle. It will lead to flagging of material and uneven stitches.

17- One mm extra lasting allowance means one percent wastage of leather, therefore do not have extra allowances.

18- To make shoes with an additional fitting you can patch the inside & outside of the last with a piece of sole leather. Dip the sole leather in water & fix it at the right position on the last. No adhesive required. It standard patches made size wise these can be reused.

19- If color fastners is poor use a hinder spray. This fixes the finish. This is a colorless spray.

QUALITY CHECKPOINTS ON SHOES-

1- Toe- part and back part should be straight.

2- Shoe should be neat and clean, so that the finishing auxiliaries should be attached properly and enhance the beauty of the shoe.

3- Shoe should not be twisted and tilted.

4- No over cementing or excessive adhesive should not be apply on the component.

5- Wrinkle should not be visible on visible part.

6- Marking should be proper.

7- Fixing or attachment of components should be proper.

8- No breakage.

9- No shade variation.

10- Proper toe- distance.

11- Proper back height.

12- Proper stitching.

13- Proper packaging.

14- Proper binding of color on shoe surface.

Quality department basically deal with maintaining the quality of footwear to satisfy customers demand. Quality control department co-ordinates with various departments to maintain the quality standard. Quality department is responsible for maintaining the good quality of product in whole organization because a good quality product enhance the goodwill of the organization in the market.

COLOR MATCHING GUIDE

The principle used in the guide to color matching is known as **Color Circle.** Circle is made with three primaries by placing it on the corner of a equilateral triangle. Rest of the color which are made by the different composition of primaries are shown on perimeter of the circle and side of the triangle.

The color- mixing process may be required for repairing, especially if the leather is in dedicated colors. It is advisable to obtain the pigments from the specific leather tannery because other pigments may not match.

In common usages word COLOUR refers to coloured or colouring substances like pigments, dye solutions color, oil paints etc. But color (more precisely the sensation of color) is the impression produced on our retinas by pencils of colored light. A substance whose particular colouration is due to certain pigments determines the colour of the body.

Local color – Every object seen under normal light has a color, which is peculiar to it. This is known as local color. Placing the body under a light can alter the local color of a body, which is it colored. For example – the local color of a lemon (yellow) may appear green in a blue light.

The primary colors are-

1- Yellow
2- Blue
3- Red

A primary color is a pure unmixed, uncompounded color made from a single pigment. There are three primary colors also called basic colors because they form the basis of all the colors whether neutral or spectral.

INTRODUCTION TO COLOR MATCHING-

Most often it is very difficult to come to an agreement between two parties when the question of color matching comes. We find each one talking in subjective aspect in some arbitrary language which results disagreements. When ever the question arises regarding the tinge of the shade, redder or greener, whether the shade is lighter or darker, there make a chance of difference in answer of different dyes. This depends upon the sensitivity of different dyers and how close they have absorbed the shade. However this is another things that both the dyers may match the same shade by using their own concept but their statement regarding a single shade may vary. This has been so for very subjective concept. Probably this is the root for the development of a proverb **"color matching is more an art than a science".**

Introduction of spectrophotometer have made an endeavor to disprove this proverb and set a counter logic in support of opposite statement that **Color matching is scientific and it needs appreciation in photo physics, photochemistry, optics, quantum mechanics, chemistry of colorants, geometry, mathematics and computer application.**

Color matching involves all the steps through which we find the color value of the shade in terms of hue, chroma, intensity, tone, and brightness and with the help of these color values we predict the proportions of binding blocks to match a given sample as closely as possible.

During selection of dyes one should have the idea about primary, secondary and territory colors and also about the result that will be obtained by addition of different proportion of primary, secondary, and territory colors.

PRIMARY COLORS- A primary color is a pure unmixed, uncompounded color made from a single pigment. There are three primary colors also called basic colors because they form the basis of all three colors whether neutral or spectral. The three primary colors are - Yellow, Blue & Red because red contains only red, yellow only yellow and so on.

All colors are resultant blend of these three primaries.

SECONDARY COLORS-

When equal parts of two of the primary colors are mixed, the color we get is called **Secondary color.** For example- green comes from blue and yellow, orange from red and yellow, and violet from red and blue. Secondary colors lie midway between the primary colors on the color wheel. They are less strong than primaries.

For example-

5 Blue + 5 Yellow = **Green**

5 Yellow + 5 Red = **Orange**

5 Red + 5 Blue = **Purple**

Other binaries from different percentage of primaries are shown on the perimeter of the circle.

TERTIARY COLORS-

When two secondary colors are mixed the color we get are called **tertiary colors. Tertiary colors consists of three primaries.**

Purple + orange = 5 R + 5 B +5 Y + 5 R = Russet (Red Grey) Being red in excess.

Orange + Green = 5 Y+ 5 R + 5 B + 5 Y = Citron (Yellow Grey) Being yellow in excess.

Green + Purple = 5 B + 5 Y + 5 R + 5 B = Olive (Blue Grey) Being blue in excess.

Similarly 5 Y + 5 B + 5 R = BLACK

In the color circle brown is lying in between orange and black. It consists of-

4 Y + 2 R + 2 B = BROWN

This can be written as-

2 Y + 2 R + 2 B + 2 Y + 2 R = BLACK + ORANGE = BROWN

Thus the brown shade is also a mixture of Black and Orange and is located between these two. It is similar to the way olive and navy blue are located.

COMPLEMENTARY COLORS-

Two colors are called complementary colors if the one consists of what other lacks in order to contain the three primary color red, yellow & blue.

For example, red is the complementary of green because-

Red + Green = Red + (yellow + blue)

The color Wheel consists of primary & secondary colors. This shows how colors are related.

Secondary color lies on the outer circle. Colors opposite to each other on the wheel will counteract each other. Thus if a mixture of color is too red for a match the addition of green will KILL the red cast. This is one of the most helpful facts in color mixing to match.

Examination of the inner circle will illustrate the problem of casts like red can tend towards blue or yellow, thereby showing a purple or orange cast respectively. In making an orange, mixing a red with a purple cast with yellow will produce a MUDDY color. However, if a red with an orange cast is used the resultant color will be a lot CLEARER. The primaries to make secondary should therefore have a cast closer to the secondary.

COLOR WANTED	**COLORS & SHADES MIXED**
Brown	**Red with black**
Tan	**Yellow & red with black**
Grey	**White with black**
Pink	**White with red**
Green	**Blue with yellow**
Cream	**White with yellow**
Orange	**Yellow with red**
Purple	**Blue with red**

To make darker add black and to make lighter add white. To make brighter add greater proportions of first mentioned colours.

KEY POINTS-

All the colors located in color triangle are based on pure yellow, pure blue, and pure red, but when ever any one of the primaries colors after combining these becomes differ.

Suppose the yellow available is slightly reddish yellow

5 Y + 5 R = Orange it will be reddish than expected **5 Y + 5 B = Green** will be contain some red brought in by this yellow which will locate it towards olive.

HOW TO KILL A COLOR-

Each secondary has one primary color missing. For instance orange is missing blue, while green is missing Red. So remove a red cost by addition of green. Similarly orange kills blue and purple kills yellow.

Yellow + Red = Orange missing blue, if blue add it kills orange.

Blue + Red = Green, missing red. If red add it kills green.

Red + Blue = Purple, missing yellow. If yellow add it kill purple.

HOW TO MAKE THE MATCH MUDDY AND CLEAN-

Governing factor to make the shade muddy or male the shade clean is the **"TONE** "of the colors that are going to be added. Suppose yellow is combined with blue that has red undertone. The color mixer will contain all three primaries and therefore the resultant shade will be **"muddy".** On the other hand if some yellow is combined with blue that has green undertone, the color mixer will produce a clear match.

Some typical combination that produce muddy color-

Red (bluish) + Red (yellowish) = Muddy Red.

Red (bluish) + Yellow (reddish) = Muddy Orange.

Some typical combination that produce clean match-

Red (yellowish) + Yellow (reddish) = Clean orange

Red (bluish) + Blue (reddish) = clean purple.

TONE (CAST)

Inclination of one color towards another color is termed as TONE. EXAMPLE- Yellow FB-G (BASF dyestuff) has greenish tone, Brown FB-R has reddish tone. Hence, the meaning is that, base color is brown but it deviates towards red.

FATTY ACID SPEW-

"Sometimes when finished leathers are chilled, the surface becomes coated with a white crystalline deposit resembling a thin film of snow. This deposit known to the trade as spew.

Usually consists of saturated fatty acids having a high melting point."

Spew is one type of fungus. All fats have a tendency to migrate through the leather when they are not irreversibly fixed to matrix. Free saturated fatty acids and all other substances are sensitive to the influence of temperature. One of temperature effects is that, it can change the substance appearance.

The most common origin of fatty spew is the migration of natural fat. At the surface the fat reaches the ends of its migration, settles and crystallizes resulting in a white layer. On processing leathers it is sometimes observed that, over same period, an undesired white milky film appears on the top of the leather. This white layer often gives rise to debates on its origine and causes, and it some cases leads to a claim for damages.

In other words- spew is where there is a temperature drop and the amount of oils, the leather can hold changes and part of the oil return to the surface of the leathers. When the leather warms up the oil will return back into the leather. This is commonly found on leather treated with oil containing **"petroleum distillation".** The petroleum distillates seem to displace the natural oil and they return to the surface.

English leather is known to spew at low temperature due to the heavy use of tallow. The spew may be removed by wiping the area with a clean soft cloth.

Spew is an undesired white milky film appears the top of the leather. The reason for the white layer is the high melting point on the grain surface. Which is about 60 degree c to 70 degree c approximately.

WHAT IS FATTY SPEW-

All fats have a tendency to migrate through the leather when they are not irreversibly fixed to the matrix. The main reason for the white spew layer on the grain is the high melting point, which is about 60 degree c to 70 degree c for all of the substances causing fatty spew. Below this temperature they begin to solidify but remain undetectable to the eye. Since they are not part of a larger structure, but free, they tend to cling to one another with decreasing temperature, this tendency to form larger structure and change their appearance.

Reason behind spew formation-

In general natural fats and oils consist of triglycerides. These components are ester of glycerol's and three different fatty acids.

For the understanding of fatty spew it is important to look at the presence of specific fatty acids in the natural fat of the skin. The most difficult ones is the longer carbon chains saturated fatty acids which are solid at room temperature but crystallize overtime.

. **C 14** (Myristic acid)

. **C 16** (Palmitic acid)

. **C 18** (Stearic acid)

This mechanism also applies to all other substances, other than natural grease, that have a high melting point.

All natural oils contains free fatty acids and a certain portion of them is present in their saturated form. The typical level of fatty acids (saturated and unsaturated) in vegetable oils amount to more or less than 1%, for animal fats/ oils to be more or less than 4% and fish oils have up to 15%.

Where does it come from? Animals.

Bovine's hides contains 2 to 4% natural grease of which 40 to 50% is unsaturated. Sheep and pig skins can contains much higher levels of natural grease percentage. An average composition of sheep fat contains up to 30% natural grease of which two third 67% consists of saturated fatty acids.

Some of the natural triglycerides are subject to hydrolysis. Hydrolysis can easily occur under acidic or alkaline conditions and also through enzyme activity.

CONCLUSION-

The amount of free unsaturated fatty acids contained in normal bovine hides is too small to cause fatty spews. The same is true for fat- liquors. Most of the fat- liquors contains free unsaturated fatty acids as chosen ingredients or byproduct from the raw material and its processing. The main cause of fatty spew, acids lies in the natural skins with a very high content of natural greases, such as sheep and pigs, where large sufficient quantities of free unsaturated fatty acids can become available and migrate to the leather surface.

COMMON FAULTS IN SHOE FINISHING-

1- Excessive polish in sponge.
2- Lacquer varnish is not of the correct quantity and shade.
3- Sponge and containers is not kept clean.
4- Sponge is sticky.
5- Line mark is visible after sponging.
6- Dirty shoes are being polished without cleaning.
7- Overflowing finishing auxiliaries and making the shoe and work table dirty.
8- Wrinkles should be visible in main visible portion.
9- Excessive or overspill adhesive should be visible on shoes.
10- Shade and grain variations on pair.
11- Socks should not be covered properly to upper and lining.
12- Counter should not be properly fitted in between upper and lining.
13- Shoe finishing should not crack after folding.

TESTING IN THE FACTORY (SHOE INDUSTRY)

The testing of finished leather or finished shoes should also be carried out on a regular basis in the shoe factory. This testing should also extend to finished footwear and machinery as part of the total quality control system.

Then a simple question arises "Why should we Test". The answer is very simple- **"It increases the quality of our product and decreases the financial loss of the industry".** So improvements should be made where necessary and should involves the following three areas-

1- Action to identify the main cause for rejects and returns.
2- Using a shoe performance forecasting system.
3- Installing process control system.

So, it is very clear that the high profitability is not necessary but the quality control is the main point. So, testing is therefore essential to keep the losses due to rejects and returns to an acceptable level and much of this testing must be carried out by the manufacturer on a routine basis. Testing is one of the tools used in quality control, a very important topic that we shall discuss in details.

QUALITY CONTROL-

The following important points of quality controls are-

1- Quality control is determined that all shoes made are equal to the quality laid down in the specifications.
2- Specification of the quality of materials and labour required must be laid down before we can inspect production to find out whether the shoes meet the requirements of the specifications.
3- We inspect to find out when mistakes have been made, but the quality control, we eliminate the cause of the errors.
4- To control quality, we must control the quality of materials, workmanship, and servicing of the machineries.

Note firstly that to control quality, we must establish specifications that cover design, materials, processes and workmanship. Such specifications must be established during the development stage before any commitment is made. Developing a shoe without testing the suitability of the design and materials may lead to a commitment to manufacture generally unsound shoes.

DESIGN AND DEVELOPMENT-

When a sample shoe has been constructed, it should be subjected to a through analysis to uncover any defects in design or construction. Thus, we can minimize the chances of premature failure in wear and reveal any characteristic likely to reduce the shoes sale-ability.

The following check list is one possible scheme for carrying out such an analysis-

1- **SIZING-** a) Marking

2- **LAST-** a) Dimensions in relation to the materials, construction, and target population.

b) Toe spring relationship to material and construction.

c) Heel pitch in relation to heel attachment and the associated components.

3-EFFECT OF THE DESIGN-

a) On the feet.
b) On the choice of material
c) On any particular component part (including the need for reinforcement).
d) On flexing areas.

4-FOOT COMFORT-

a) Effect of the positioning of cut- outs and decorative stitching.
b) Flexing area and the associated concentration of creasing in wear.

5-CONDITION OF WEAR-

Will these impose any particular stress concentrations and if so, will the components and construction satisfactorily withstand it?

MATERIAL CONTROL-

If bad materials are used, good work serves no purpose. As this is costly, materials for production must be of optimum quality. If a specification is agreed with a supplier, the customer has a right to expect this specified quality in the product.

How can this consistency be checked?. The only way is by inspection. Using the order and the specification, incoming supplies should be inspected for

1- Quantity
2- Size- range
3- Quality
4- Price

Because leather deliveries have tended not to conform to specifications, the following details of a leather delivery should be checked.

1- Does it tally with the order description for type and color?
2- Is the total quantity correct?
3- Is the footage marked on the individual hides correct?
4- Are the substances received as ordered?
5- Are the shades of color correct and do they match throughout the delivery?
6- What are its cutting values?
7- Is it of the correct quality?
8- Is it invoiced at the correct price?

Leather testing is divided into three types- Physical testing, chemical testing and finish testing. Chemical testing should usually be done in a laboratory, but a number of physical and finish tests can be carried out in a factory.

SOME IMPORTANT QUESTIONS REGARDING FINISHING-

1- Mention the type of finishing materials, their characteristics and uses?

2- Mention the different types of waxes in brief and their uses in shoe finishing?

3- What are the characteristic of Nappa leather? Devise a system of finishing for this leather explaining the suitability of nappa leather?

4- Fill in the blanks-

a) ---------- Leather is velvety leather with velvety effect on grain side.

b) --------- Wax is recommended on cotton for nappa leather.

c) ----------- improves colorfastness of resin finish.

d) Finish break can be repaired to some extent in protein finished leather using---------.

e) ------------- finish burns on excess application on heat.

5-Write short notes on-

a)- Carnauba wax

b) Cotton roller

c)- Burnish finish

d) Patent leather

e) Split suede leather

f) Oil pull up leather

6- What remedial action will take as finishing in-charge, if

a) Burnish bleeds

b) Whiteness occurs on finished shoe.

c) If the shoe after finishing is not having sufficient gloss.

d) Shade variation in shoe made of dyed nubuck leather.

e) Fungus appears on leather surface.

7-Define the following leathers.

Aniline leather

Burnish leather

8-Short answer questions-

a) List out point wise the main characteristics of smooth corrected grain leather.
b) List out point wise the main characteristics of nubuck leather.
c) List out point wise the main characteristics of burnish leather.
d) List out point wise the main characteristics of brush off leather.
e) List out point wise the main characteristics of aniline finish leather.

9-A company has received an order of 25,000 pairs of moccasin shoes to be cut in buff full grain burnish leather.

Size assortment is given below-

5	6	7	8	9	10
2	2	2	3	2	1

Material consumption per pair 2 sft. On grade C leather. Company has received 48,000 sft. Of leather. Later on it was realize that the materials ordered is less in quantity. How much materials needs to be ordered again? If you receive the left quantity buff snuffed burnish what recommendations you will give to the cutting and finishing in charge?. Discuss in brief.

11-Finishing is done to give the value addition in product. Justify the statement giving suitable examples.

12-Describe in brief four systems of Leather repairing.

13-Describe five faults of shoe finishing work mentioning their causes and remedies.

14-Write the characteristics of the following leather and establish finishing system based on the characteristics.

a) Cow hair cell printed
b) Buff burnish weidge
c) Cow Smooth
d) Sheep Napa

15-State whether the following statements are true or false.

a) Burnish leather is glossy leather.

b) PU film coated leather is as good as synthetic material.

c) Hard cream can be used as a base coat.

d) Oil pull up is two- tone effect leather.

e) Burnish is wax- finish leather.

16-Short answer question.

a) How will you stop the hungriness of leather in shoe room?.

b) Name three types of corrected grain leather commonly used for upper making.

c) List out different liquid dressing and their application procedures.

d) List out important characteristics of aniline finish leather to be considered by shoe finishers.

17-Write down ten quality checkpoints of shoe finishing.

18-Give a flow diagram of the two systems of finishing work in brief.

19-Justify the statement value addition and cost deduction by finishing.

20-Discuss in brief shoe faults their causes and remedy.

21-Discuss in brief leather faults and their impact and rectification in finishing.

22-Discussin brief wrinkle chasing and dressing techniques in shoe finishing.

23-Discribe five faults of shoe finishing work mentioning their causes and remedies.

24- Write short notes on-

a) Filler **b)** Soft cream **c)** Hard cream **d)** Carnauba wax

25- Mention the different types of waxes and their uses in shoe finishing.

26- What is spew?. Explain the reason behind spew formation. How this problem can be overcome?.

27- Discuss various type of finishing materials available and their specific uses in brief.

28- A company in Noida has received an order of 25,000 pairs of slip on shoes to be cut in buff calf F/G burnish brown color. Lining is D/D buff lining in beige color and sole is of TPR. Thread used is 20/3 and 60/3 nylon beige 3 ply threads and there is a steel buckle on the saddle. The company supervisor has recommended finishing system, which is given below- Lasted upper +P1-S (brown) + heat setter(120 degree)+ iron at 60 degree+ cutting with high pressure at high speed+ cutting again high speed burnishing wax+ other lasting operations+ p29 brown+ cutting at high speed + polishing at low speed. The manager is somehow not convinced with the system. Evaluate the system given above and give your recommendations.

29- Mention the different types of cleaners their objectives and their uses in shoe finishing process.

FINAL INSPECTION OF FOOTWEAR-

It is normal practice in the footwear industry to inspect pairs at the end of the process. The following guidelines will help ensure that the inspection is done correctly.

1- Do not inspect unless there is an approved sample signed by the customer.

2- A technical specification sheet for each style approved by the production manager/ customer.

3- Sufficient light should be available on a clean table. Lighting levels should be 1300 lux.

4- A list approved by the production manager showing major & minor defects should be available in cutting/ closing/ lasting department. The general rule is that no major defect is allowed, only 2- 3 % minor defects should allowed. Without a list of major and minor defects no inspection is possible. In case a major defect occurs not listed in the defect list the quality controller should not be blamed. This new defect should be added to the list for future lots.

5- Keep a tape, scale 12" & 6", scissor, crepe rubber piece & stitch gauge with you always.

6- Inspect plan wise and keep track of size wise pairs passed as shown in the chart below-

Plan no. Model no-. Color----

NO. OF PAIRS------

Size	6	7	8	9	10	Total
Order Pairs	1000	2000	3000	2000	2000	10,000

This chart immediately gives the ratio and status of inspection size wise & ensures that wrong sizes are not send.

7- Major defects should be destroyed or punched through so that they are not recycled or mixed with good shoes. Keep the defective shoes with you till get replacements.

8- Keep track of defects as shown in the quality inspection report. This report gives number of pairs defect wise. Look for the top three defects & take steps to correct them immediately. Stoppage of production could also be done of such measures. If the same defect recurs for 3 days the quality control system has failed & the quality control inspector is responsible.

One should remember that recording of defects is not the main job. Corrective & preventive action is the main job of the quality control inspector.

9- Take a 10 minute break after every two hours otherwise inspection fatigue occurs. During these periods go to the line & look at ways to correct quality problems.

10- A shoe must be inspected by looking at it with the toes facing you and with the back strap flack seam facing you. Shoes must inspected pair wise always.

11- Have a 10 minute discussion daily with production supervisors about major problems & how to correct these. If these are not attended to, stop inspection & report to the production manager.

12- Quality inspectors suddenly change standards of inspection when a complaint is received. Many times he rejects up to 70- 80%. This is simply ridiculous because with such a high rate of rejection it means that the quality control system has collapsed and the quality control inspector is responsible.

13- The following charts must be clearly displayed at the quality control table

    a- Back height chart

    b- Major & minor defects list

    c- Key points raised by the customer if any

    d- Approved sample

    e- Defects file

14- Keep a defect file for each customer. Whenever a complaint is received keep a copy in this file along with corrective and preventive action taken. The purpose of this file is to catalogue defects and ensure that they do not recur.

15- Final inspection by itself is not enough. This must be supported by laboratory test reports on materials and the final shoe. Fit and wear trials help immensely in quality control.

16- Remember that final inspection is only a postmortem. It is much better to spend time in process quality control. The rule **"Do it right the first time"** is to be always followed.

HOW TO CONDUCT EXTERNAL INSPECTIONS TO FOOTWEAR

Many customers send their representatives for final inspection or use organizations like SGS to do the inspection. This procedure covers fully packed consignments.

1- Inspection can only be done on the basis of an approved sample & technical specifications from the customer.
2- A copy of the order should be available with packing instructions.
3- A copy of the invoice should be available showing style wise quantities & colors. Packing lists should also be available.
4- The consignment should preferably be kept in an inspection room with cartons stacked serially as per packing list.
5- Count number of cartons to ensure that there is no shortage.
6- Check the quantities of the two lowest and two highest sizes of the order physically if an order is from 5- 11 sizes check quantity of sizes 5, 6, 10, 11 physically. Since these are edge sizes quantities will be small and can be checked easily. This is to prevent any packing mistakes.
7- Draw samples for inspection as per random sampling table.
8- Draw pairs for inspection in all sizes.
9- Keep a list of major & minor defects and inspect shoes and tabulate results on the inspection sheet.
10- Take one pair at random and send it for lab test for following tests-
    a- Sole adhesion
    b- Sole abrasions
    c- Sole flexing
    d- Cold crack if shoes going to cold climates the test is done at 20 degree C.
11- Seal cartons checked with special tamper proof tape. Keep record of cartons opened and sizes checked.
12- Check carton labeling, boxes, box labels to ensure that they are as per order.
13- Issue certificate if the quality is satisfactory.
14- In case tests for PCP, Azo dyes are required do these tests before issuing certificate.

TEST CRITERIA FOR VISUAL EXAMINATION

1- **Restitution of the last shape**

Longitudinal profile

Crow section

Toe tip

Heel seat

Upper close

Stand of the shoe

Point of tread

Heel position

Heel pitch

Side pitch

2- **Upper and lining material**

Uniformity of color

Uniformity of glaze

Dirt and smudge

Visible material defects

Wrinkles

Loose grain

Mechanical damages

Sticky

3- **Bottom material/ bottom part**

Uniformity of color

Uniformity of texture

Uniformity of glaze

Dirt and smudge

Visible material defects

Susceptibility of breakage.

4- **Seams-**

Type of stitch
Stitch density
Edge distance
Stitch pattern thread
Tension needle hole
Mechanical damage.

5- **Preparation of upper-**
Skived edge
Folded edge
Edge inking

6- **Assembly of upper-**
Position of parts
Seam securing thread
Mechanical damages
Distortion of parts
Off- set of parts upper
Edge work-up lining
Work up heel lining
Work-up upper cutting outs.

7- **Lace fastener-**
Eyelet hole
Reinforcement
Shoe laces
Hook eyelets
Lace strip .

8- **Hook and loop fastener-**
Version
Adhesive length
Attachment

9- **Elastic gusset stretchable length-**
Tying

Seam looking

Band incorporation

10- Zipper-

Running ability

Coverage

Incorporation look

11- Buckles-

Attachment

Firmness

Attachment abrasion

SHOE ASSEMBLY-

Vamp length

Back height

Upper closer

Lasting wrinkles

Pressure marks

Grain coating

Grain cracks

Traces Distortion

SHOE BOTTOM-

Heels cover Sole

Cementing Sole

Arching position of top piece

Sole finish

Heel attachment

Insole wrinkles

Top piece fastening.

TESTING AND QUALITY ASSESSMENT

Leather finds place in consumer's articles in its natural form after being subjected to certain finishing treatments. These finishing treatments such as staining, polishing etc. are done more for imparting an eye-appeal rather than for modifying the basic properties of the leather themselves. The physical characteristics of leathers namely, strength, elongation, porosity, absorption, flexural endurance, compressibility and resilience, fastness to light, weather etc. only a combination of two or more properties is to be tested to ensure the quality of the leather for a particular use. For example, sole leather are to be tested for water absorption as well as resistance to abrasion. Upper leather for flexural endurance, fastness to rubbing, water vapor permeability etc. belting leather for tensile strength and elongation. The physical and mechanical properties to be determined on a given sample of leather must have relevance to its ultimate end- use.

Testing equipments and test methods (developed for different styles and designs of footwear) are numerous. At the same time the units of measurement of different properties for the same test method also varies from specification to specification. For example most of British Standards (BS) are in FPS system where as DIN (German Standards) are in SI units. Test procedures and testing equipment of Bally (Switzerland) and **Shoe and Allied Trades Research Association (SATRA) UK** and specification of **British standards (BS).** German standards (DIN) and **International standards (ISO)** are widely used. A minimum requirement for any shoe industry or a testing laboratory are specified here.

UNIVERSAL TESTING MACHINE-

As the test specimen is pulled, it is acted by tensile force. The length of the specimen increases. The specimen is fixed in between two jaws and pulled. The load required to pull is increased automatically on a dial gauge calibrated in lbs or kgs. The increase in length is measured using a scale. Similarly when a test sample is compressed as in soling material it is possible to measure compressive load. Universal testing machine the latest being computer aided INSTRON, is a versatile equipment for various test methods involving tension and compression. The equipment consists of a main frame, two columns of this frame support a moving crosshead. Load cells of different values 5, 10, 50, 500 kg and so on could be mounted on the top and below for compressive force. The load cells are strain gauges. As the force is exerted (tensile or compression) the resistance of the strain gauge increases or decreases accordingly. The increase or decrease in resistance is calibrated in terms of load (lbs. or kgs). Grip to hold the specimen are attached to the cross heads. The movements of the crosshead can be stopped at the preset load, or preset elongation. Computer aided mechanism controls various machine operations like constant loading rate, speed of cross head, cycling etc. Data is processed automatically, and the test results are documented and obtained on a graphic printer. A number of test methods are developed, on this machine. For example, load and extension, tensile tests, slit tear test, tongue tear test, peel strength of adhesives, breaking load of threads and so on.

TENSILE STRENGTH-

"Tensile strength is the force (kg) per unit area of cross- section (sq.cm) required to cause a rupture of the test specimen".

Test sample of standard dumb-bell shape are cut, parallel and at right angles to the back bone in case of leather, warp and weft directions in case of fabrics and coated fabrics. The thickness of the sample is measured. Area of the sample= width of the sample x thickness.

The test sample is inserted in between the grips of the universal testing machine. The rate of the separation between the jaws is set usually at 100 plus or minus 20 mm per minute. When the specimen breaks, the load is recorded

Tensile strength = Breaking load / Cross sectional area

Guidelines- Leather- A tensile strength of above 150 kgf / cm2 for grain leather and 100 kgf / cm2 for split leather.

Coated fabrics- A breaking load of 7.0 to 10.0 kgf/ cm.

EXTENSION TO BREAK-

The sample is gripped in between the jaws. The distance between the samples is measured. The test piece is elongated until it breaks. The elongation increase in length when the sample breaks is measured.

$$\text{Extension (\%)} = \frac{\text{(Final length at break – Initial length)}}{\text{Initial length}} \times 100$$

On a computer aided machine the load and extension curves are drawn automatically on t

Guidelines- Percentage elongation without break of leather 25 – 30%.

Coated Fabrics- 5- 10% depending upon warp or weft direction.

TEAR STRENGTH-

"Tear strength is the load in kg required to tear the sample of leather of unit thickness (cm)".

Leather specimens (50 x 25 mm) provided with a slot having the specified dimensions or a straight cut of 20 mm length for light leathers are used for determining tearing strength.

Sampling is done both parallel and perpendicular to the backbone and the mean thickness of the test specimens determined. Tearing is accomplished at the dynamometer using a test piece holder and the maximum recorded load is noted.

Tearing strength, kg/cm thickness= Tearing load (kg) / Thickness (cm)

All leathers meant for the fabrication of footwear and leather goods like upper leather, clothing leather, and gloving leather are tested.

Guidelines- Coated fabrics 50 N (DIN)

Leather- 35 to 120 N depending upon source and thickness (DIN).

TONGUE TEAR STRENGTH-

" The load (kg) required to tear the leather beyond the cut made perpendicular to its surface, expressed per unit thickness (cm)of the test specimen is the tongue tear strength".

Two thirds of the length of the test specimen (75 x 25 mm) is cut, the mean thickness of the remaining one- third portion is determined and the sampling is done parallel as well as perpendicular to the backbone. The tearing load is determined using the dynamometer.

Tongue tear strength, kg/cm thickness = Tearing load (kg) / Thickness (cm)

Applications- All leathers meant for the fabrication of footwear and leather goods.

For coated fabrics- 26.6 to 4.5 kgf.

BREAKING STRESS- STITCHED UPPERS-

Samples are cut out of stitched upper. Vamp and toe, vamp and quarters ans so on. The test piece is mounted on instron/ tensile tester with one end clamped in one jaw and the other end in another jaw, the row of seams in between. The load when the stitches fail is noted.

STITCHING THREADS-

Various properties of stitching threads like Breaking load, extension at break. Tenacity and tightness are tested by the universal testing machine.

Breaking load is determined by clamping the specified length of the thread usually 500 mm in between the bollards. Bollards are special grips used for clamping threads. The machine is started. The load and extension is recorded. From the graph, breaking load in kgf, percentage elongation at break, tenacity (Breaking load/ weight per unit length of thread) x 100, can be calculated. Tightness is the load required to produce different extensions at 2.5%, 5%, 10% and so on.

PEEL STRENGTH OF AN ADHESIVE-

Two strips each of dimension 150 x 25 mm are cut out of the materials to be bonded. The surfaces of the adherends are prepared similar to the conditions required, before the application of adhesive. Over an area of the strip measuring 75 x 25 mm at one end of the prepared surface of each strips, adhesive is applied by means of a brush. When the adhesive surface is dry, another coat of adhesive is given. When the adhesive surface is dry, test the surfaces by means of a finger, for tack, and align the coated surface of the strips face to face carefully in such a manner that the free ends of the strips lie in the same direction. Press the specimens at a pressure of 2 to 4 kg/ cm2 for 30 to 60 seconds. The two strips of the sample is gripped in between the clamps of the tensile tester and separated at a uniform rate of 5cm/ min to obtain the peel strength of the adhesive.

HEALTH AND SAFETY

In finishing operation, a lot of water and air pollutions are observed in atmosphere. It is created due to presence of solvent chemicals in top coat operations. Basically, it should cover four main points-

--- Health risks resulting from exposure to solvent hazards at work.

--- Solvent fire and explosion hazards.

--- Principles of prevention

--- Emergency procedures employed

HEALTH RISKS-

The use of nitro cellulose lacqour and thinner damage the lungs of the working people, because both are solvent base. The effects of solvents can be acute or chronic depending upon concentration and length of exposure to the body. Main effects are irritation and allergic to skin, eyes and respiratory tract.

FIRE HAZARDS-

Solvents are highly flammable. Solvents in the work place are major fire and explosion hazard. The improper storage, handling or transport may result in minor fire to major disaster resulting in loss of human life.

Fire in principle needs three elements to survive-

1- Fuel
2- Heat
3- Oxygen

To check any fire hazards these elements should be controlled. In this respect it is important that the organization should use water base top coat in place of solvent base top coat.

PRINCIPLES OF PREVENTION-

It should base on organizational as well as operational control.

Four basic principle of operational control are-

1- Eliminate the hazard- replace as far as possible, solvent based chemicals to that of water based.

2- Put a distance/ shield between the solvent and worker. The term being sprayed must be kept within the work area of spray booth and there should not be over spraying. The inhalation of fumes is dangerous and can be avoided by using a proper spray booth, spraying technique and wearing a mouth cover.

3- Provide general and local ventilation near spray booth with exhaust fans and running water to reduce concentration of airborne contaminants such as fumes, gases, vapors and mists.

4- Protect the workers by using personal protective equipment like dust mask respirators, protective goggles, gloves etc. Water based and spirit products, mainly the spirits, degrease the skin if kept in contact for a prolonged period of time. Use of after work creams are suggested.

5- Spillage, disposal, cleaning. Major spillage of solvent products should be immediately soaked by dust or sand to prevent spreading and in particular to avoid contaminating drains.

BASIC STEPS OF SHOE FINISHING

FINISHING WITH THE HELP OF THE FLOW DIAGRAM-

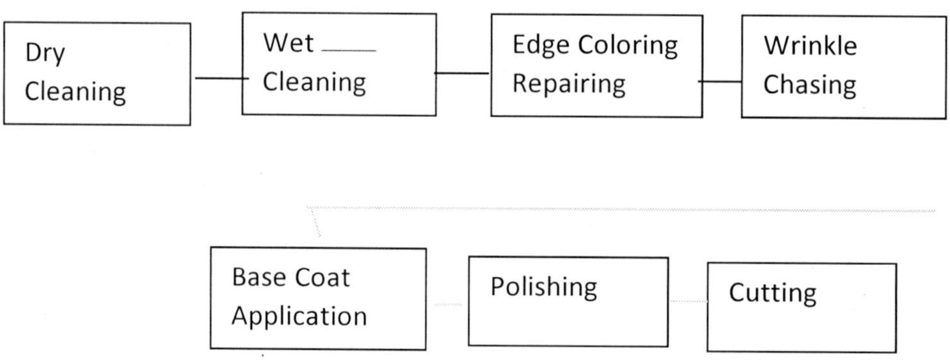

ALTERNATIVE METHOD

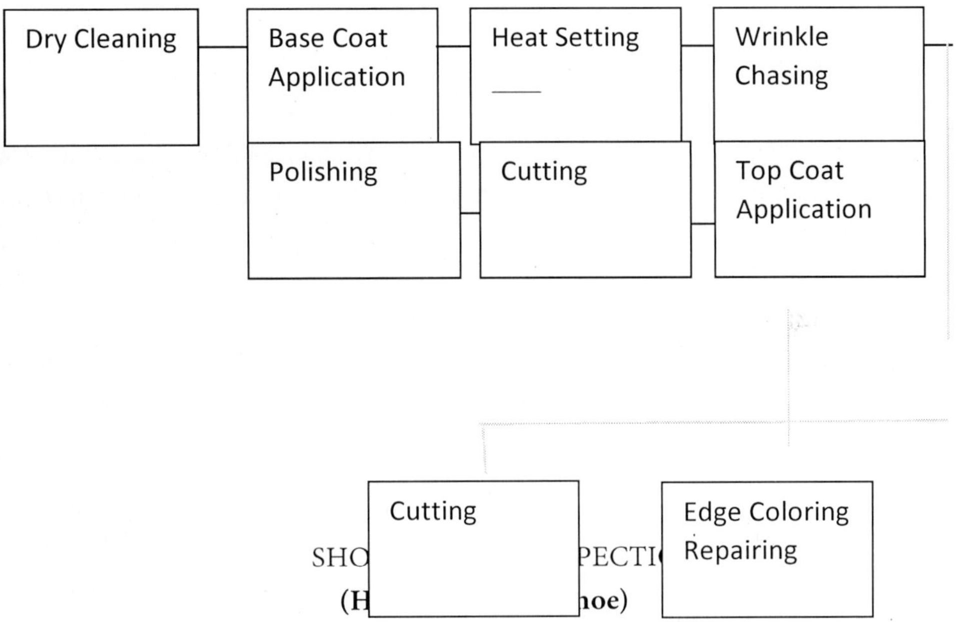

SHO PECTI

(H hoe)

You will never look at shoe the same way again---------- once you know how to professionally inspect a pair of shoes. Quality is a very important feature of any pair of shoes you might make, buy or sell.

Knowing how to run a shoe quality inspection is a critical skill for shoe designers, developers and product line manager. When a new sample arrives it is critical to inspect the materials, assembly technique and workmanship. Inspecting a shoe is a great skill to have as a shoe buying customer in a store. So here is how to grade and inspect a shoe like a professional.

"A" grade shoes-

Shoes with no functional defects or cosmetic defects that will impair the marketability of the shoe. These are high quality shoes, its appearance and look is beautiful and fit correctly. An A grade must follow the production specifications and match the approved confirmation sample.

"B" grade shoes-

Shoes that have no major functional defects that will not cause injury to the person wearing the shoes. These shoes may have cosmetic defects or little production mistakes or workmanship issues that can not be properly repaired. These will be discounted and or diverted to markets more tolerant of cosmetic defects.

"C" grade shoes-

Have major functional defects that could cause injury to the wearer or major cosmetic defects that cannot be repaired. Shoes are also considered C grade if they have poor workmanship or materials defects that could soften the normal life expectancy of the shoe or damage the organization reputation.

HOW TO INSPECT A SHOE-

The main points in an inspection are as follows-

1- Is this the correct shoe, a matched pair?
2- Is the shoe clean?
3- Does the shoe follow the specification?
4- Is the workmanship high quality?
5- Is the shoe damaged in any way?

Let's inspect a shoe –

The first step in any inspection is to review the shoe packaging.

1- Is the shoe in the correct inner box for exact model?
2- Is the box presentable? Make sure the box is not damaged or dirty.
3- Is the box is correct size? The shoe should not be crushed inside a small box.
4- Confirm the information on the box end label matches the shoe color/ model/ size.
5- Check any hangtags to make sure they are correct for the shoe.
6- Remove the shoes from the packing box. Do you have a left and right?.
7- Are the shoe same size & color?
8- Check the shoe tongue label information.
9- Does the pair really match in length?
10- Now check the alignment of the shoe parts – starting from the front roll the shoes to align the parts, toe caps, vamps, overlays, eye stays, eyelets etc.
11- Check upper side by side compare finish and colors of each part.
12- Make sure the shoes sits on the outsole straight. Check that the upper is not rotated off center.
13- Check the back height and collar lines match.
14- Look midsole side wall for wrinkles.
15- Check seam joining the upper to the out sole.
16- On shoe bottom check for color bleeding between color blocks.
17- Check to make sure the outsole parts fit together neatly with no extra glue.
18- Color matching of the shoe parts (suede, nubuck and natural leather).
19- Upper wrinkles.
20- Check rough trimming or rough cutting.

A complete inspection means the shoe is checked inside and outside. In inside inspection we must see the lining is clean and have no wrinkle. Run your hand around the collar, feel for any lumps or glue. For leather shoes look out for any lasting nails or staples. For sports shoes sure the footbed is straight, level and fitting correctly. Too small the footbed will more slide around, too big the footbed will be wrinkled.

Next inspection the tongue lining for wrinkles. Run your hand down inside to check the vamp and toe cap from inside. Feel around the toe along footbed for lasting wrinkles. Feel for any rough stitching inside.

HOW TO CLASSIFY QUALITY DEFECTS IN SHOES

Shoe manufacturing is a rough process. A lot of manual and mechanical operations are done during the processing. Even well made pairs will eventually show signs of wear and tear with constant use. Hence the manufacturer are responsible for managing quality defects in shoes, so that customers are satisfied with the finished product.

The quality defects for shoes are generally sorted into one of the following three categories-

1- Defects that fail to meet mandatory regulations to the user are typically classified as **"critical defects".**

2- Defects that made the footwear unacceptable by affecting appearance, durability and stability are called **"major defects".** A major defects found on a shoes is not acceptable by customer or even customer returning the pair.

3- Defects that are lower than the desired quality standard but are **not likely to result in customer dissatisfaction,** product return or complaints are called **"minor defects".**

CLASSIFICATION OF DEFECTS-

Most shoes can be divided into two parts. First is upper part and second is bottom part. Upper part is generally the most important area in terms of visual appeal because it is the area most apparent to the customer or wearer. Bottom part is less important because it includes areas of the shoe that are obvious to the customer.

Any defects found is upper part that is more noticeable and more likely to be considered a major defects. The same defect found in bottom part is more likely to be classified as a minor defect.

1- **EXCESS GLUE, WAX OR OIL-** Excess glue, wax or oil marks are among the most common quality defects found in shoes. These types of residue are especially common because-

a) Most of shoe production facilities use adhesives and other chemicals during production.

b) Factory workers are less likely to protect against or remedy like excess glue, wax or oil when rushing to complete an order.

Glue, wax or oil residue can often be cleaned off without difficulty, otherwise it damage the appearance of the product and render a shoe unsellable. Excess glue, wax and oil marks are often found in both upper and bottom areas.

2- WEAK CEMENTING-

A cementing material for shoe (adhesive) is generally used when applying the sole to the upper part of the shoe. This defect is generally found between the join line of upper and bottom. This type of defect in the shoe industries is called major defect.

Prevention-

It is important to make sure that the factory manufacturing the footwear is using the correct type of adhesive. But the more common cause of weak cementing is not enough adhesive applied between the shoe components. **Make sure workers are using enough adhesive but not too much.**

3- ABRASION MARKS-

Abrasion marks are a type of quality defect in shoes that normally appear on upper part. These are often considered more serious when found on leather shoes or those with a glossy surface because they are more obvious. This marks are usually caused by poor handling by factory workers during the production process.

4- ASYMMETRY IN SHOES-

In line with other soft lines asymmetry can be an issue where different components of shoes do not line up as they should. Some examples are commonly found on a shoe or pair of shoes are-

a) Where the sole of the shoe does not line up with the body from a front, rear or side view.
b) Where certain parts of the shoe are not straight, such as the tongue etc.
c) Where part of the one shoe is higher or lower than the same part of its component in a pair.

Issues with shoe symmetry should be addressed with the manufacturer. The best way to find symmetry in shoes is to **place them side by side or back to back.** You need to determine whether or not the shoes reflect each other in terms of **Height, width, colour** and so on. For example- if you place shoes back to back, you need to observe that the height of the heel is the same on each one, otherwise you have a defect.

5- INCORRECT SIZING-

Due to an error during the production process, the shoe was labeled and packaged with the incorrect size. This should be considered a major defect because shoes that does not match specifications for size are likely going to be unsellable.

Prevention-

Incorrect sizing is usually a result of the way the finished shoes are sorted and packaged. Naturally, shoe sizing discrepancies are more common in factories that are disorganized. And often all that's needed to prevent incorrect sizing is better procedures for handling, packaging and sorting the finished product. Taking a look at a factory's warehouse and packaging areas can tell you a lot about the likelihood of incorrect sizing.

6- NAIL OR SHARP POINT-

Nail or sharp point is among the least common quality defects in shoes on our list. This is not a visual defect, so it does not apply to upper and bottom part.

Some shoes, especially those are made with leather, have nails to bind the sole of the shoes to its upper part during production. If these nails are not properly pressed down, they can protrude into the insole, creating a sharp point that could hurt the consumer. In other cases, a needle might be mistakenly left in a shoe.

Prevention-

Most of the footwear and garments industries should generally equipped with metal detectors. After production is complete, workers set the units on a belt that runs through the machines to **look for needles or other sharps nail** that might have been left by mistake.

Factories should also have **QC** staff examining shoes off the line for signs of sharp points that could be harmful to the end- consumer. If sharp point are found in your order or shoes, the factory needs to investigate which process is responsible and eliminate the cause.

CONCLUSION-

Shoes can be bought to make a fashion statement or simply provide utility and comfort. Most shoes are manufactured with some level of quality in mind. And as a customer or manufacturer, it helps to look out for some of the common quality defects in shoes that could affect you or your business.

UP- GRADING OF SHOE UPPER LEATHER IN FINISHING

POLISHING-

Polishing is used in order to close the surface and to equalize the absorption of the crust leather. Some crust is very sensitive to polishing and tend to become loose. The application of an oil or an oil emulsion helps us in two ways-

----- The oil keeps the grain softer.

----- Due to the penetration of the oil the shade of the crust intensifies. This characteristics is very helpful for the finishing of dark and even black articles. Before application you must ensure that the oil does not highlight any defects.

OIL- COATS-

If the absorption of the crust is very uneven, an oil coat helps to level out the penetration of the following application. If it is not enough use some hydrophobing additive into the base coat, but do not make the pre- coat too water repellent as insufficient adhesion or flow problems should occur in next step.

CATAIONIC PRE- BASE-

Lots of pre-base coats are based on cationic products. Their advantages on cationic crusts is that only a thin layer, a very good sealing is achieved. Since the cationic products do not highlight open defects of the crust as much, a very equal surface is achieved while keeping the natural aspects of the leather.

SEALING PRE- BASE COAT-

Sealing pre-base coat for corrected grain leathers follow another philosophy. In this method, snuffed grain is restored using soft resins which remain on the surface, and additives ensures both sealing and rewet ability. A solid film should not be created on the leather. This would lead to a double- skinny finish.

After plating the base coats should neither build up too strongly nor penetrate into the leather too much. This means that the adjustment of the pre- coat for corrected grain shoe upper leathers is very important and also very much dependent on the crust leather.

BASE COAT-

In base coat operation generally we prepare thin film. Hence the solution viscosity should be high and the solid content of the solution should low. This leads to a reduced penetration and prepare a thin film. The choice of binders and additives are important and require fast covering, filling additive or fillers to be used. If the final article requires medium gloss, a high amount of silica- based fillers can be used. Some duller have to be used since lower the gloss level of the base, the better the up- gradation. About 50% of the filling effect can be achieved by silica based products, the remaining 50% must be achieved by using waxes and oil emulsions. It has also the property of filling agent.

FINISHING EFFECT

1- ANILINE LOOK-

In order to achieve high aesthetics a natural aniline look is of great importance. After the leather is base coated and ready for the final top coat or even before the last base coat application, the time is right for an effect coat. It can be base coat mixed with some aniline dye, a separate coat based on aqueous emulsion lacquers with an aniline dye. This coat will intensity the shade and also improve the transparent look of the finish. In this way the leather is covered but the aniline dye makes the leather look more natural.

Effects are limitless. This effect coat can be applied un- evenly to make the surface equally uneven. Which can improve the up-grading, because while grain defects are obvious on an even surface, they can be hidden by applying clouds or by a design roller. An effect on leather can be done from the crust up to the top coat, and applying two- tone- effect on the crust leather as well as on the base coated leather.

2- WAXES AND OILS-

On crust leathers effects such as burnishing, pull- ups, Crunch or antique effects are possible. All of them have in common the creation of a uniform unevenness. Grain irregularities are not covered by these effects but very effectively hidden.

For all the wax and oil related effects on crust leathers, a very even uptake is important. Depending on the crust and its tanning/ re-tanning, different products may show different behavior.

3- PULL – UP LEATHERS-

In order to adjust the shade of pull- up leathers, tinting is common before applying the pull- up oil/ wax. For the oil pull- up leathers with their typical soft pull- up effect, a high up grading is hard to achieve. Most important is to avoid uneven penetration of the oil and to avoid highlighting defects, such as open scratches, tick marks or pin holes. It is helpful to apply a barrier based on an oil emulsion before the pull- up oil or to apply a strong penetrating oil from the flesh side. It is the most important to find out the right oil suitable for the crust and the demanded effect. If a strong effect is demanded, a strong darkening oil is necessary and ensure the defects are not highlighted significantly. For the lighter pull- ups the idea of the barrier is very helpful.

Aqueous wax emulsion are a highly effective barrier. This procedure is important for wax pull- ups, where a sharp and pronounced effect is demanded.

Very often the water- based wax emulsion is applied at first followed by a pull- up wax. Depending on the final article this wax coat is either plated, polished or an adhesion coat. The adhesion coat is needed for waxy leathers that have to be finished, in order to guarantee sufficient adhesion for the subsequent finishing coat. A lot of these leathers are made with gloss or even high gloss top coat. The finishing coat should not be too thick as that would decrease the pull- up effect and its re- polish ability, nor should be plating be too hot.

Even for the high glossy leathers plating too hot is not advisable, as the pull-up products could migrate into the top coat, which could lead to a grayish tinge undermining the gloss.

Overall, waxy crunch effects or anti- pull- up effects, have a big upgrading capacity. The leathers usually get a final milling until the desired effect is reached.

4- BURNISHING EFFECT-

Burnish is one type of special wax which provide dark polish effect. Some articles are delivered without the final polishing, so that after manufacturing the shoe is given a hard polish to pronounce the shape of the shoe or just to upgrade it with a fashionable look. Some leathers get their final polishing before the shoes have been made.

This polish does really upgrade the leather. A very attractive optical effect together with an intensive shade and a natural gloss will be achieved by this finishing.

For more upgrading and in order to match the color, some pigments or dyestuffs can be added to the burnish wax coat. But this will not increase the wet rub.

5- ANTIQUE EFFECTS-

Antique effects can be made on both full grain and corrected grain leathers and also on splits. For splits a short- fibered crust is easier to finish and the effect will also be more elegant.

The upgrading potential with such an effect is pretty high. Due to the regular unevenness of the two- tone effect most of the grain defects can be hidden on the full grain leathers and corrected grain leathers and the splits get a high fashionable appearance. Different opinions are possible-

----- A thin and hard dark pigmented coat can be applied and partly removed either by milling or any other mechanical action.

----- A hard, dark pigmented resin is applied to the leather, which creates a cracking effect during drying.

----- A light base coat is applied and after wards a darken very lightly sprayed, non- stretchy coat is applied. The darken coat will crack when the leather is stretched and the lighter shade appears.

After the desired effect is achieved it has to be fixed and protected by a clear or slightly colored binder coat. Any top coat can be used in order to finish the article.

Very closely related to these antique effects are the high glossy crystal effects, mostly used on splits and corrected grain leathers. The important point here is the very high gloss of the remaining particles on the leather and these particles should be very small. The resultant is a suede or nubuck leather with a glossy shinning just like a crystal.

To achieve this effect the coat must not penetrate too much, must have enough adhesion to ensure the effect does not disappear overtime. The application is done by spraying, better one or two light coats than one heavy coat. If the crystal effect is sprayed in one thick layer it is hard to get a suitable effect afterwards.

To increase the gloss and to smooth the surface this crystal coat needs a hot plating. Careful milling will produce the high glossy coat, but it can feel rough.

NAPPA LEATHER

Nappa leather is a full – grain leather and it should be soft and pliable un- split leather from sheep, lamb, kid skins and sometimes pig, cow and calf. It is generally used in high class of garments and quality home furnishing. It is a high pricey leather. As a pliable and soft nature, it develops a pleasing finish with age. With its intact top grain, it does not retain moisture and breathes better than cheaper leathers. **It is considered a premium grade of leather.** In spite of being soft, it is both durable and strong. You can find nappa on home furnishings of the highest quality such as expensive desk chair, high quality of garments (both male and female) different types of accessories, bags, footwear and ladies under garments for cold countries and baby skirts. Nappa leather is available in different thickness, different colour, and different finishes as per the requirements of customer.

SKIN QUALITY-

Nappa leather in the general term for particularly soft, chrome tanned, smooth leather of all animals skin types and fields of use. A distinction is made between natural, slightly pigmented, pigmented and sanded leather. Natural nappa leather is known as aniline leather. It is open pored and imbued with aniline colorants.

Only the highest quality skins are chosen for nappa leather. The leather does not contains scars, bug bites, scratches or other physical imperfections. Because of the quality of the hides chosen to nappa leather, the material itself is more expensive because it has young cattle and tight grain pattern without defect.

Sometimes people refer to forms of full grain leather as nappa leather, but each company has its own way to making nappa leather.

Taken from the top layer of the hide, where all the grain is full grain leather develops a natural look with age and use.

ANILINE NAPPA- Very precious and very sensitive-

The natural characteristics of skin material are well visible because they are not covered by pigments and coatings. Therefore, the leather must not be damaged by tick- bites, thorn scratches or other external causes. For this reason, this material is often very precious and expensive.

Aniline leather are extremely sensitive to dirt and fat, as well as to bleaching out caused by sunlight due to the fact that the leather is pores are not sealed. Just like aniline leather, slightly pigmented nappa leather is dyed through with water soluble colorants to which pigments were added which makes the material more resistant to light and abrasion. Additionally, the surface appears to be more even.

A colour coat makes nappa even and insensitive-

Both kind of nappa leather are water- vapor permeable and therefore provide an excellent heat exchange. With pigmented nappa leather, colorants are applied firmly to the grained leather's surface by using a binding agent. This makes the material less breathable but at the same time easier to clean and less sensitive to dirt. Nappa leather that has been sanded on the grain side gets an extremely smooth surface when colorants are applied.

FINISHING IS AN ART THAN SCIENCE

Finishing is more of an art than science and requires patience and skills, which can be achieved by a perfect mirror finish. Usually the final touch is by hand. When we upgrade the leather we do the different operation like snuffing and using different hand tools. Finishing is the process that removes all visible contaminants on grain surface and creates a smooth and shiny surface. A process of abrasion accomplishes the desired polished finish.

The finishing of leather is probably the most complicated and least understood phases of the industry. It has been more and more art than science. Finishing leather is not simply a matter of painting the surface to cover up the mistakes of the previous operations or to improve it by concealing scratches, it contribute to the durability and beauty of the leather and must be an integral part of the process. The compatibility of materials, tanning, colouring and fat-liquoring all play an important role in the character of the leather and kind of finish it will take. The finish system is a compromise between conflicting effects. If coverage of the defects is the main problem some of the grain beauty will be lost. If resistance to scuffing is desired there is a danger of having a stiff varnished look. Each of these conflicting properties must be balanced in the final finish system.

ADHESION-

When the finish is applied, it must stick, for this reason the leather surface must be " wettable". A top finish need not adhere to the leather itself, but it must stick to the base coats of the finish to prevent peeling. Leather finishes requires extreme flexibility and stretch. Finishes that do not have good adhesion and good flexibility will peel and crack.

STABILITY-

Leather may be exposed to extreme heat during the manufacture of a shoe. When the shoe is worm in cold weather, extremely low temperatures may be encountered. Thus the film must have a wide- range of temperatures over which it is soft and pliable, it must also be hard to maintain the high gloss which is required. The leather must be able to stand up to a reasonable amount of both wet and dry abrasion and to be re-finish with ordinary shoe polishing methods applied by the customer.

COATING TECHNOLOGY-

Coating may be classified as-

1- Lacquer systems
2- Drying oil systems
3- Condensation systems
4- Latex system

1- LACQUER SYSTEMS- The formation of the film is based on the evaporation of the solvent containing a film forming material (nitrocellulose dissolved in an organic solvent).
2- DRYING OIL SYSTEMS- These are natural drying oils such as linseed which will undergo polymerization upon drying. This is different from lacquers in that the setting of the film is not simply a deposition of the high molecular weight material, rather it is a chemical reaction taking place between the dissolved film-forming materials and atmospheric oxygen. In the drying oils the film forming materials (a binder) is an organic chemical having a high degree of instaurations. As the oil absorbs oxygen from the air, the unsaturated material is oxidized and reactive portions of the fatty acid molecule develop which can then polymerized with other fat molecules to form a continuous film on the surface.
3- CONDENSATION SYSTEM- The formation of the film is due to a chemical reaction between the various components of the finish after application. The reaction may form a plastic or polymer in water between two molecules. Such systems are usually heat activated and may be backed, glazed or hot pressed. Condensation is used in leather industry through proteinaldehyde reactions and with other resin systems. In this

kind of finish the reactive components are usually mixed shortly before application, due to the limited pot life of the components.

4- LATEX SYSTEMS- In this system the binder used is emulsified in water. When the latex is applied the water evaporates or sinks into the leather and eventually a phase inversion takes place. A continuous layer of the binder spreads on the surface of the material being coated and becomes a continuous film. This film can be diluted with water, enabling thin films to be applied. The latex systems and dispersions of resins in an emulsion form are widely used in preparation of leather finishes.

TYPES OF LEATHER/ FOOTWEAR FINISHES AND SUGGESTED CARE

A variety of finishes are used to enhance the natural beauty of the leather. Aniline finish is like staining wood allowing the natural grain to shine through, pigmented is like painting – completely covering the natural surface. Nubuck is the top or grain side of the leather which has been buffed with a fine sand paper to give it that velvety appearance.

The most common finishes are aniline, semi- aniline, pigmented, patent, metallic, oily, waxy, suede and nubuck.

The manufacturer select leather of a quality standard. When leather is cut, special precautions are taken to minimize damage and waste. The leather is then assembled and all the pieces are again inspected for quality.

Leather permits the free flow of air and moisture, making it an ideal material for footwear. Because of the special nature of leather, it is most important that you receive product care information when making your purchase.

NAPPA- Nappa is a very soft, thin and good texture, pliable and silky feel leather generally used for manufacturing garments, leather goods, clothing, baby skirts for cold countries and hand gloves. It is the full grain leather drummed to give a soft and comfortable feel. Use **zorbel** to clean and condition.

SUEDE- Flesh side of the leather that is buffed and brushed. Can be made from any of the leathers, has the nap raised by a buffing/ snuffing process with the help of fine grid paper to bring up a fine velvet like finish. For this type of leather use **zorbel** to clean and condition.

NUBUCK- Grain or smooth side of leather, buffed with an abrasive action giving a velvety surface finish. Suede and nubuck are similar products, so use **Lyddy joseph** to treat them. By using this you will provide protection from water and stain marks, making the shoe or garment water repellent. If your nubuck or suede shoe has been neglected or is really dirty, you can use **Glycerine saddle soap.** The whole shoe must be shampooed. Firstly, wet the shoe all over. Apply the shampoo into the surface and using a soft shoe brush in a circular movement work in the shampoo, then rinse well. Let the shoe dry naturally, away from direct sun light or heat. When the shoe is dry brush with a suede and nubuck brush or wire suede brush then apply **water and stain protector or water proofer.**

PATENT, PLASTIC, POROMERIC OR "WET LOOK" UPPERS- Patent leathers have a surface coating of PVC or polyurethane to give a very high gloss finish. The treatment is used for high fashion footwear, but has the disadvantage of reducing the ability of leather to breathe and release perspiration.

Care products- Remove soiling by wiping with a damp cloth and **JOSEPH LYDDY GLYCERINE SADDLE SOAP** to give added brightness.

ANILINE- Leathers treated with a clear aniline dye and wax finish to allow the colour and natural grain pattern to show through. This process gives a very natural appearance to high grade shoes.

Care products- Water and stain protector or water proofer to water proof.

SEMI – ANILINE- Transparent dyeing with additional fine spraying with pigment color to equalize and irregularities.

Care products- Water and stain protector or water proofer to water proof.

REPTILE- The skins of other animals and reptiles are used in minor quantities.

Care products- To care for these leathers you should use the products recommended for the care of aniline and semi- aniline leather.

MIGRATION AND BLEEDING IN FOOTWEAR AND LEATHER GOODS PRODUCTION-

Bleeding terms relates specifically to the running of colors. It is often used to transfer of substances between materials in contact with each other. Migration refers to displacement of a compound within the material or from one material to another by diffusion at the molecular level. In **bleeding,** the compounds rise to the surface and thus are able to leave their original environment. In the case of **migration,** the compound are able to make their way through the material to the new site, however far away that may be. They are sometimes to cross several materials or several different layers of differing natures before arriving at their end destination. In practice the distinction between bleeding and migration is not always easy to make. We will using the term **"bleeding"** for running of colors and " migration”

for internal transfer.

HOW TO STOP LEATHER SHOES FROM BLEEDING OR STAINING-

If the shoes are real leather and the suede side is unlined inside the shoe, the friction of your socks or skin while walking will rub the red dye until there is no excess dye remaining to rub off. The solution has been started which is wearing a dark sock.

Sometimes when the insides of the dyed leather shoes become dampened by sweat, excess pigment can leech out of the leather and cause staining on your feet or socks. However, a more immediate solution is to waterproof the leather so that the moisture from sweat will not be able to reconstitute the dye. Leather water proofers come in the form of sprays, creams and pastes. Sprays are the most convenient and easy to use, but creams and pastes often contain wax and oil for simultaneously conditioning your leather.

SPRAY WATER PROOFERS-

STEP- 1- Wipe down the insides of the shoes with a slightly dampened cloth to remove dirt and residual sweat. Dry the shoes before applying the water proofer.

STEP- 2- Spray an even coat of water proofer on the insides of the shoes. Make sure all areas are covered. Allow the water proofer to dry.

STEP- 3- Re- apply water proofer to the shoes regularly to maintain protection from moisture.

PASTE OR CREAM WATER PROOFER-

STEP- 4- Wipe down the inside of the shoes with a slightly dampened cloth to remove dirt and residual sweat. Dry the shoes before applying water proofer.

STEP- 5- Fold up a clean, soft cotton cloth and dab one end into the paste or cream. Rub a liberal coat of the water proofer on to the inside of the shoes. Re- dab the cloth in the paste or cream as needed.

STEP- 6- Re- fold the cloth to expose a clean side. Work the water proofer into the leather by rubbing in circular motions while applying firm pressure.

STEP- 7- Use a clean, soft cotton cloth to remove any standing water proofer then wait 12 hours before wearing the shoes again.

STEP- 8- Re- apply water proofer to the shoes periodically to maintain protection from moisture.

REMARKS- Always apply a protect ant to your shoes before wearing them, this product seals the fibers of your shoes to prevent a color transfer. Look for a **"water proofer"** product, as repelling water, in addition to dyes, is often one of the main benefits of this type of shoe protectant.

Avoid bleaching bleeding unless the instructions specifically mention bleach. Bleeding dyes usually occurs on bold to dark coloration which may become splotchy or otherwise visually damaged with the use of bleach. For existing marks, use a suede eraser followed by a suede brush to remove spots on suede shoes or apply a paste made of baking soda and water to spots on canvas shoes, rubbing until the stain diminishes, remove the paste with a dry cloth.

REFERENCES-

1- Finishing handout- FDDI
2- International project- TTLM in LIDI Ethiopia.
3- Net searching

About the Author

Footwear is more than a simple wrapping or protection of the foot. The notation that shoes indicate a great deal about the person's taste and their identity. Shoes have for centuries given hints about a person's character, social and cultural place. Shoes are powerful things as they take control over the physical and human space in which we live. They are the principal intersection between our body and physical space.

The theme of this book is to provide fundamental concept of leather and shoe finishing, so that this knowledge will be helpful for personnel those who opt. leather, leather goods and footwear finishing as their carrier.

R. D. Singh acquire his B. Tech. in Leather Technology from H. B. T. I. Kanpur (U. P.) Kanpur University, and M. B. A. in (Production Operation Management) in UPRTOU Allahabad. After serving the leather industry he has deviated towards the teaching line in F. D. D. I. as a Junior Consultant (Footwear). He is an examiner and paper setter of U. P. Technical Board, Lucknow (U. P.). He has 36 years experience in Leather industry as well as Footwear industry.

There have been very few text books written for students of the Leather & Footwear industry in recent years and it is therefore a particular pleasure to welcome this book. I can be reached at rdayalsingh1961@gmail.com / rdsingh@fddiindia.com or mobile no. 08420921428 or 09628775989.